Stopping Traffic

Book I
Love at the Crossroads series

BY
PAT SIMMONS

Other Christian titles include:

The Guilty series
Book I: *Guilty of Love*
Book II: *Not Guilty of Love*
Book III: *Still Guilty*

The Guilty Parties series
Book I: *The Acquittal*
Book II: *The Confession,*
Fall 2015

The Jamieson Legacy
Book I: *Guilty by Association*
Book II: *The Guilt Trip*
Book III: *Free from Guilt*

The Carmen Sisters
Book I: *No Easy Catch*
Book II: *In Defense of Love*

Love at the Crossroads
Book I: *Stopping Traffic*
Book II: *A Baby for*
Christmas
Book III: *The Keepsake*
Book IV: *What God Has*
for Me

Making Love Work Anthology
Book I: *Love at Work*
Book II: *Words of Love*
Book III: *A Mother's Love*

Single titles
Crowning Glory
Talk to Me

Praises For Pat Simmons

I love Christian Romance novels and Pat Simmons knows how to unlock the imagination and take it on a quick path of hope, love and Jesus. You will always find some sort of message in her books just like I found in Stopping Traffic. I smiled! ...*Tamara Gatling, reader*

Pat Simmons does it again and again!
Another great story from Pat Simmons! What I love about her books is they are all biblically based! She shows how we, as humans, are in need of healing, deliverance, forgiveness, etc. I really like her approach to the dating scene! It is refreshing from some other Christian novels that allow their characters to engage in sexual activity without being married! Thank you, Pat, for giving us some good, pure, interesting Christian materials to read!! I appreciate you! You and a handful of other Christian Authors are rare commodities in these last days! ... *LeeLee, reader*

Simmons has laid it all out on the line in this installment of the Jamieson legacy. This is pure Christian romance with a touch of heritage. There were moments in the middle that I wanted them to get it together but it turned out better than expected. The personal touch of genealogy is wonderful and will make you think about your own family heritage. Wanted to see more Grandma BB but loved the new

character development. Simmons is on top of her genre...
Reviewed by M. Bruner "Deltareviewer" on Free from Guilt

Free from Guilt may be listed as Christian fiction, but it's so much more. You read about family history, romance and transformation. This is a great read and leaves the reader wanting more, with that being said I'm looking forward to the next Guilty installment... Reviewed by Melody Vernor-Bartel for Reader's Paradise

Jeremiah 29:11 KJV

For I know the thoughts that I think toward you, saith the LORD, thoughts of peace, and not of evil, to give you an expected end.

Chapter 1

"A crossing guard?" Candace Clark wanted to cross her eyes at the snippy woman's request. Surely she was joking.

Apparently not, as Mrs. Lovejoy's fingers hovered over the computer keyboard, anticipating Candace's compliance. Sitting smugly behind a massive desk, the Duncan Elementary School principal had definitely seen too much sun during her summer vacation. The tan on her face was somehow darker than her neck and arms.

"Yes, it's the only slot that's lacking volunteer participation. Since you missed early registration, this is all I have left." Mrs. Lovejoy seemed to take pleasure in reminding her. She grinned, displaying teeth that needed a sun bleaching application.

Candace twisted her mouth like her daughter sometimes did when she was trying to get out of something she didn't want to do. *Weren't upper classmen vying for that coveted position?* she thought. Well they could have it! Candace schooled her expression so as not to give away her contempt at performing the task: no brow lift, eyes roll, or huff.

PAT SIMMONS

The petite woman across from her was killing all her joy. As a matter of fact, Candace had had an abundant supply of jubilance when she walked into the cramped office that would have better served as a library with the numbers of books lining the wall-to-wall shelves.

"What about..." Candace paused. She strained her brain. "I could act as back up to a lunchroom mom. You know, two moms are better than one?"

Mrs. Lovejoy's dumbfounded expression made it apparent that the woman's patience was running thinner than her body frame. Squinting at the wall clock behind Candace, the woman gave her a pointed look.

"A teacher's assistant?" Candace pressed.

Shaking her head, Mrs. Lovejoy's lips formed a "no" moments before she said it. "No."

Well, she had another think coming if she thought Candace was going to do that grunt work. Nobody in their right mind would want to volunteer to get sunburned, take a shower without soap in an unexpected downpour, or have their teeth chattering because a strong wind just slapped them.

The scenarios were endless. Nope. Mrs. Lovejoy was just going to have to tap someone else for that position. She wasn't even an outdoors person. She liked central air in the summer and a blasting furnace in the winter. Plus, she had another good reason for turning down the job.

This was all Candace's fault. She had been too preoccupied with other important last minute tasks, like making sure her daughter, Lindsay, had her immunizations, including a physical, purchasing every school supply Lindsay could wrap her hand around, and making sure all accessories matched her uniform.

2

With so much on her mind, she had forgotten about the packet of important school forms that had to be signed, which included the mandatory parent volunteer signup sheet. And still there were countless things left to do before school started.

She didn't want to come across as difficult, but "no" was about to roll off the tip of Candace's tongue when her daughter leaned forward.

"Mommy, you'll be like a policewoman and all the cars will have to stop."

The angelic expression, worshipping eyes, and hopeful smile on her daughter's butterscotch face made Candace grit her teeth. She wouldn't put it past the principal to have given her daughter some kind of hand signal, that only kindergarteners could decipher, to put on that, "Please, Mom" face. "A crossing guard is not a law enforcement officer, sweetie."

Lindsay pouted, which was comical. The girl's long dark brown natural hair was confined in colorful barrettes that complemented her jumper. As an only child, it was hard for Lindsay not to be the apple of her eye. The things she did for her baby.

Truthfully, Lindsay's first day of school would be bittersweet. They had never been separated for a long period of time since the day Lindsay was born. Her best friend, Solae, called her overly protective, but that was Candace's prerogative.

"All right," Candace mumbled quickly before common sense and fear talked her out of it. "What's my shift?" *After all, thirty or forty minutes once a week wouldn't be so bad*, she tried to talk herself into it.

"Excellent." Mrs. Lovejoy clapped her hands once and

displayed the first smile since their meeting began. Actually, it looked more like a smirk. "We need you at the intersection of Cougar Lane and Lindbergh an hour before school starts and if you can, come back again before classes let out, say at 2:45."

The woman was pushing it. "Okay, what day?"

Sifting through folders, Mrs. Lovejoy hesitated. It was the first time she'd avoided eye contact. "Right now... Monday through Friday." She appeared sheepish. "We're having trouble filling those spots."

Imagine that. Candace kept that sentiment to herself.

"But," she rushed to explain. "Hopefully that won't interfere with your work hours. I'm sure it will only be temporary. That is, until other parents sign up."

She was accustomed to juggling her priorities to make things work, but for a daily crossing guard position? It was a good thing her boss had five children himself. He and his wife shared participation in school outings and meetings. Otherwise, he might not be sympathetic to her predicament.

After five years of working from home as a virtual assistant for Kendall Printing in order to be close to Lindsay, Candace looked forward to interacting with adults face-to-face. Her employer was flexible with workers' schedules, but for five days? She would ask and hope for the best. Granted her work week was only thirty-five hours, but she was required to abide by the schedule, even if it meant she had to bring Lindsay with her before or after school to finish a project.

Candace stood to leave after signing the form. She reached for Lindsay's hand.

"One more thing, Miss Clark," Mrs. Lovejoy stopped

her. "I see you didn't complete all the information on your Parent section. Regardless of whether the parents are married or not, we want to encourage dads to become involved as well. Are you single or divorced?"

"I'm a widow." Candace swallowed. It still pained her to utter those words. "My husband was killed…while crossing the street. An inattentive driver talking on a cell phone didn't see him until it was too late."

Walking out the office with Lindsay in tow, Candace felt she had said too much, but it was in the forefront of her mind, given the circumstances. Still pondering her qualms about being a crossing guard, she couldn't help but wonder… since God didn't stop the traffic for Daniel to get safely out of harm's way, would He make the cars stop for the children?

"I'm cool," Royce Kavanaugh defended his single status for the umpteenth time to the three members of his brotherhood of firefighters. His name always somehow surfaced whenever they hung out at I-Hop for breakfast after working the last of their four day, twelve-hour shift.

He was the only one who wasn't married, didn't have a current girlfriend or hadn't fathered any children. Therefore in their eyes, he was basically living a lonely existence. But Royce had no problem being the odd man out.

"You haven't seen Marsha yet," Felix Noble, their fire truck's driver or chauffeur, winked, then shook his head. "If I wasn't married to her cousin, I'd take her out. She has all the assets that drive a man crazy. She's looking for a hero."

His grin hinted at mischief.

"Hey, my sister is first in line. Brenda's been inviting "hero" over here to dinner for months, and he has yet to accept." Lt. Allen Johnson eyed Royce while backhanding Felix in the stomach in jest.

At the start of his career four years earlier, Royce was cocky enough to think of himself as a hero with his good looks, muscular build and the firefighter's uniform that seemed to drive women crazy. They flirted with him, ever so casually invited him into their beds and were always eager to provide him with an endless supply of home-cooked meals. That only served to feed his already large ego.

On the flipside, his job had caused his last couple of ladies to rebel against his absences at Christmas, anniversary parties, barbecues, you name it. Although his heart was in the right place; he wanted to be with them at each function, but the life of a firefighter was unpredictable. So far none of his ladies had stayed around long. One by one they'd cite feeling neglected as the cause and would stop answering his calls. With no shortage of beautiful women at his beck and call, though, he just kept the cycle going.

Then something happened to change his pompous attitude. It came with his first defeat as a firefighter. His best efforts hadn't been good enough when he rescued a child from a burning house. The little boy never recovered from the smoke inhalation and passed away. That young death caused Royce to search for a deeper meaning of life.

Not long after that, Royce did a one-eighty and surrendered his life to God's perfect will, which led to changing his mindset, lifestyle, and his revolving-door dating habits. Plus, he had seen Allen's sister. Not only did Brenda cook all the time, but she ate most of what she prepared, too. Her pretty smile and hazel eyes weren't enough for Royce to close his eyes and pretend she was physically attractive. Royce was a leg man and Brenda had enough for two women.

"I've turned my matching-making over to God," he advised before eying Captain Hershel Kavanaugh, his older brother by four years, inviting him to chime in and come to his rescue. The two only resembled each other in small ways: in their charming smiles, medium brown skin color and height—six-three.

"Hey, I'd rather they pick on you than me. I have done just fine rearing my two boys without the help of a woman," Hershel defended, a single parent through no fault of his own.

Hershel's ex-wife was the perfect example, in Royce's mind, of what would happen to him if he picked the wrong one. Much wiser after his failed marriage, his brother was very cautious about who he allowed to spend time around his sons. Neither brother was interested in just dating for dating's sake.

"Listen, man, my sister would be happy to feed their hungry bellies…" Allen wouldn't back down as he turned his attention to the captain.

Royce exchanged glances with his brother. Turning to the lieutenant, they said, "No," in unison.

When Hershel asked for the check, the waitress smiled. "The ladies at that table," she pointed to a booth that was crammed with four beaming beauties, "already paid your tab." She added in a whisper before walking away, "They said it was for your services."

Everyone at his table waved their gratitude, but Royce didn't linger on the women's smiles or winks, nor did he want to engage in small talk, knowing that some of them might hope it would turn into pillow talk. At that moment, he was much more interested in getting some sleep.

As a practicing Christian, Royce no longer desired to have just any warm body beside him when he slept. Instead, he was all right with cool sheets and a clear conscience. As they headed out of the restaurant together, Royce's thoughts were focused on the type of woman he was praying would come into his life, a special someone who would love God first and appreciate him for himself, not just his looks or the uniform he wore.

Chapter 2

Candace was still sulking about her assignment to crossing guard duty as she dressed for church. Her feelings were a mixture of fear and defiance.

When she arrived at Jesus Saves Church, it seemed as if God was waiting for her.

"You should never think you're in too high a position to reach down, to do a menial task to someone in need...." Pastor Rodney Alexander preached to a packed congregation.

"There's no room for selfishness or vain conceit in a Christian's heart. When we put others before ourselves, it's called humility.

"How can we get blessed when we don't bless others? Philippians, chapter two reminds us that the greatest people among us are supposed to serve the least of us. "

She was getting the message loud and clear. Her pastor's electrifying sermons were always encouraging, uplifting, and at times, mixed with humor, but today Candace was getting a spiritual whipping when she reflected on her puffed up spirit in Mrs. Lovejoy's office on Friday.

True, she did lack a spirit of humility for not wanting to perform what she considered a menial task, but she knew Jesus understood her anxiety about crossing the street. Fear overwhelmed her so much so that it took her twice as long to get to the other side of the street as other pedestrians, thinking about the fate that Daniel had suffered.

She had unconsciously developed a routine of double checking both directions before stepping off the curb, concerned that she and Lindsay might suffer the same tragic end.

Her friend called it a ridiculous ritual, but she just couldn't help herself. When Candace drove and came upon someone who was walking across the intersection, she reduced her speed even though she seemed blocks away. "God, You know I don't want to have this anxiety, please help me," Candace had quietly pleaded countless times since her husband was killed.

I have not given you a spirit a fear, Jesus whispered 2 Timothy 1:7.

When Mrs. Lovejoy inquired about her marital status, Candace should have simply answered that she was a widow and left it at that. There really had been no need for her to disclose how Daniel died.

A jab in her side snapped Candace back to the present. Another nudge made her frown at her childhood friend sitting on the pew beside her.

"Altar call. Stand up," Solae Wyatt-Palmer mumbled. She had never been married, yet for some reason her mother felt Solae should have two names like Keisha Knight-Pulliam, the actress best known for her role as Rudy on The Cosby Show.

Embarrassed that she had been caught drifting through

the rest of the sermon; Candace got to her feet and straightened her dress. But she had gotten the message in a nutshell: Fear not, you have been called to work unto the Lord as a lowly crossing guard.

"This is the most important part of the service," Elder Alexander reminded the congregation. "Not the singing, the preaching or the offering. It's all about repentance. This altar call moment is about your soul. God is recruiting repenting hearts.

"You can sign up here. Don't be satisfied with just visiting churches or praying every now and then. Go all the way with Jesus and accept the baptism in Jesus' name and receive His Holy Ghost..."

Tears began to stream down Candace's cheeks. Wrapping an arm around her, Solae whispered, "Are you all right?" She nodded and leaned into her best friend.

Their life experiences had mirrored each other's until the day that Candace got married. Although Solae dated regularly, she still had not been able to find the right one. Not long after Candace had a baby, Solae had a hysterectomy at twenty-six because of gut-wrenchingly painful fibroid tumors. Candace had grieved longer than Solae before accepting the fact that her dear friend would not share the joy of bringing a precious son or daughter into the world.

The table of heartbreak then turned on Candace when Daniel was killed. Solae was just as devastated as if it had been her husband. To say they were lifelong friends was an understatement. They loved like siblings and even argued like sisters, but at the end of the day, they had each other's back.

"God was speaking to me today. He convicted my heart."

"You're not alone, sister. I've been struggling with judgmental issues, too," Solae confessed as she released her. She always reminded Candace of a younger version of Nia Long.

"Not you." Candace grinned as they shared a chuckle.

"Girl, they need a prayer line just for us," Solae whispered, pulling out a couple of tissues from her purse. She handed one to Candace.

After the benediction, Solae accompanied Candace down the corridor that connected to a chapel where children's activities were held during service. As the honorary godmother and auntie, Solae always had a treat for Lindsay, which earned her hugs and kisses.

When Lindsay saw them coming, she grabbed her picture which had been torn from a coloring book of Biblical characters. Jumping up and down, she waved furiously at Solae and grinned at her mother.

Candace rested a hand on Lindsay's shoulder to restrain her energy. She admired her daughter's artwork, a neatly colored picture of King Solomon.

After a squeeze and a kiss on the cheek, Solae asked Lindsay if she was excited about attending school the next day.

Bobbing her head, Lindsay took a deep breath and got on a roll, "Auntie, my teacher's name is Mrs. Davis. I got a lunchbox, new shoes…" she rattled off an endless list while Solae listened patiently. "Mommy got her some new clothes, too. We're going to match tomorrow. She'll look so pretty."

Lindsay gave her mother an adoring smile. Candace tweaked her nose, making Lindsay giggle.

"Who wears red on the first day at a job?" she mumbled to Solae.

"You will," she answered quietly, smiling for Lindsay. "While you're at school having fun, your mom is coming to work with me, and we're going to have fun, too."

Solae was responsible for getting Candace the virtual assistant position at Kendall Printing in the first place. Her friend had also put a bug in their boss' ear about Candace applying for the account trainee program that would be starting up in a few months. Since the promotion wasn't available for telecommuters, it couldn't have come at a better time for Candace to make the transition from home to the office. To be eligible for the position, she had to shadow someone for six months.

With a concerned expression, Lindsay frowned and tilted her head. "We didn't get Mommy a lunchbox."

"Don't worry about your Momma. I'll make sure she eats." Solae reached for one of Lindsay's hands as Candace grabbed the other and steered her toward the exit.

"Okay," Lindsay said in a singsong tone.

"Enjoy your debut as crossing guard extraordinaire tomorrow...God's given you the victory. Otherwise, He wouldn't allow Satan to taunt you. You'll be fine." To lighten the mood, Solae gave her an encouraging thumb up. "I should drive by and take pictures."

Candace rolled her eyes at the last statement. But feeding on Solae's confidence in her, she was psyched and felt encouraged. "Hey, I've got this." They swapped kisses and hugs in the parking lot.

"Bye, Auntie." Lindsay waved, then latched onto Candace's hand and skipped the short distance to their car. "Tomorrow's school, Mommy, and I get to wear my new shoes."

"I know." Candace tugged on one of her daughter's

curls and helped her into the car seat in the back of her Kia. *And tomorrow will be the first day we'll be separated for hours, the first day I've had a job outside the home since you were born and my inauguration as a crossing guard.*

It was definitely a day she hoped to endure without drama. If Candace could survive two out of the three, she'd deserve a medal.

Chapter 3

"Come on eight o'clock." Royce yawned. He was ready to go home.

After doing a twenty-four hour shift, he was beat. Usually, he worked twelve hour rotations, but he was covering for someone else. *Thank You, Jesus for that*, Royce whispered, referring to the fact that North St. Louis County had been quiet throughout the night.

While his brother finished up the new work schedule for the office, their chauffeur was checking the equipment for the morning shift. Stretching, Royce could hardly keep his eyes open as he studied for a promotion test at Hershel's urging.

Royce had nothing but respect for his sibling, who had worked and studied hard to earn his rank as captain while rearing his two small boys, ages three and five, on his own. It was overwhelming, to say the least.

Maybe it was a blessing that their mother was deceased so as not to witness the demise of Hershel's marital union. It would have broken her heart, but she would have pitched in to help, with the boys, especially. But Hershel had employed a faithful housekeeper who had been a godsend with her flexibility and genuine love for his sons.

The older generation of Kavanaugh men married for life, tracing back to his great-grandfather. Royce's generation was questionable, though. Only their youngest brother, Trent, was still happily married to his wife, Julia. The couple was blessed with an adorable baby girl.

"The engine's ready to go," Felix said, entering their shared sleeping quarters.

Snapping out of his musing, Royce did his best to look busy. Lately, every chance his colleague got, he ribbed him about going out on a blind date—no thank you. Definitely not with one of Felix's referrals.

If Royce ever found the right one—she had to be pretty enough, sweet enough and Christian enough to complement him—then he could boast that blissful state. Exhaling, he didn't know when that was going to happen. Although he wasn't in a rush, God said it wasn't good for man to be alone.

Thinking about the lack of intimacy, Royce smiled. Yes, Father did know best. Stretching, Royce rolled his shoulders and rubbed his lower back. In two long hours, he would be off work and not long after that, collapsed in his own bed.

"Wake up!" a tiny voice echoed in the background. Candace ignored the intrusion as she snuggled deeper under the covers.

Then her bed started shaking. "Mommy, I'll be late."

Candace jerked up. She blinked, disoriented,

recognizing Lindsay's panicked high-pitched distress call. Finally, seconds later it registered. It was the first day of school and work. She glanced at the clock. She must have slept through her alarm.

"Oh no!" Wrestling with her covers, Candace scrambled out of bed. "Of all days…" She had to get her daughter and herself ready, and cook breakfast. Padding across her hardwood floor, she swung open her door about to check on Lindsay.

She froze before the first step. Lindsay skipped down the hallway, modeling her red jumper. Having removed her head scarf, each of her four ponytails remained neatly in place. Candace sighed in relief that she had one less task to do. The only thing that needed tweaking was switching Lindsay's tennis shoes to the right feet.

"How long have you been up? Why didn't you wake mommy sooner?" Candace didn't wait for answers as she hurried into the bathroom. Thank God she had taken a shower the night before.

In record time, she had slipped on her red sleeveless coatdress and black sling back pumps. Solae always argued that bright colors complemented her skin tone. After a quick glance in the mirror, Candace agreed, although decked out in a red as bright as a fire truck wouldn't have been her first choice.

In the kitchen, Candace hurried Lindsay through the most important meal of the day. Reluctantly, she left dirty dishes in the sink. She ushered her daughter out of the door, grabbing her new briefcase—compliments of Solae, a black jacket for the office chill, Lindsay's backpack, lunchbox, and everything else she had lined up on the countertop near the door.

While en route to Duncan Elementary, Candace prayed she wouldn't be late for her duty at school in addition to overcoming her fear for the sake of the children and herself. That's when she remembered she hadn't greeted God.

"Lord, thank You for waking me up and all the blessings You have in store for me and my baby today. Lord, help me to be grateful and humble in Your eyesight. Amen."

"Amen, Mommy."

Candace peeked at Lindsay in her rearview mirror and smiled; she didn't realize her daughter was listening. Finally, she arrived at the intersection of Cougar and North Lindbergh. She saw a group of children heading to the corner. Candace parked haphazardly, taking up almost two full spaces. She unbuckled their seat restraints and jumped out. She didn't have time to take Lindsay to class beforehand as she had planned, so her daughter would have to stay with her until after the bell rang.

After snatching the red neon vest off the backseat, Candace turned up her nose at the worn item, then remembered the Sunday sermon. She slipped it on. "At least it matches," she mumbled and got the stop sign out the trunk.

As the children reached her corner, Candace impatiently pressed repeatedly on the button to change the light. Her heart pounded as she reminded herself she could do all things through Christ that strengthened her. Some cars slowed as the light flashed from yellow to red. When one SUV screeched to a halt, Candace jumped. She frowned at the offender for rattling her nerves. *God, please protect these children—and me.*

Taking a deep breath to recover, Candace stepped off the curb. She walked into the street mustering up confidence as she held up the sign, hoping drivers would honor it for the children's safe passage.

She breathed a sigh of relief with each group that successfully made it to the other side. The eagerness on the small children's faces was priceless compared to the sluggish stride of the older students. After a couple of waves and thank yous, Candace relaxed and began to feel like a pro—almost. She chided herself on almost missing an opportunity to serve others like church ushers, teachers, doctors and other community leaders. God had proven she could do this.

As Candace stood in the intersection, a blaring siren in the distance grew louder. Eying the countdown on the post, she ordered the children to hurry. It took God's might for her not to panic and freeze in the middle of the street. With them safely tucked behind her, and her legs feeling shaky like Jell-O, the truck whizzed by.

Despite the noise, and her mind being elsewhere, Candace thought she also heard a muffled high-pitched whistle. That irked her. She was risking her life for the sake of these children and someone had the nerve to ogle her?

"See, Mommy, you were like a policewoman. You made everybody stop," her daughter cheered, interrupting her mental frenzy. The pleased expression in Lindsay's eyes after the last group of students was safely on school property made her feel foolish for her thoughts.

"Come on, sweetie. Let's get your things from the car, so I can walk you to your first day of class."

Physically, Candace had survived; but mentally, she was still praying that another parent would surface at the last minute and relieve her of her duties. While some people feared driving across bridges or riding in airplanes, her fear was on the ground, at a corner and getting from point A to point B on foot.

Chapter 4

The air between Royce's lips just escaped, but he had no problem owning up to the whistle. Even with passing her by in a blur, he could tell she was a sight he wished he could see. The crossing guard's nice legs could halt traffic without the benefit of a stop sign.

If the crew hadn't been racing toward the scene of a two alarm blaze, he would have pleaded with the lieutenant to make a U-turn as if they were riding in a sports car, rather than a ten-thousand pound ladder truck.

No, that stop sign definitely wasn't necessary as she hurried across the street with the children. *Wow.* A chance glimpse at her face proved she was gorgeous.

Her skin was a rich combination of light and dark. Definitely a rich milk chocolate and her shoulder length hair blew in the wind as they raced by her.

There wasn't enough time to catalogue all her features, but in seconds, Royce glimpsed lips, nose and eyes. Thank God for twenty/twenty vision. From the cab of the truck, Royce shook his head. He hoped the other three firefighters with him didn't hear his blunder.

Ordering himself to re-focus, Royce pushed the vision

of loveliness to the back of his mind. His company was heading to a situation that was top priority. "Jesus, please spare both lives and property. Whatever is lost, I know You can restore, in Jesus' name, Amen."

As the fire truck sped to their destination, Royce spied the dark smoke spiraling upward and dispensing into the air. They were still blocks away from assisting the first unit on the scene, but with smoke that dark, he doubted the fire was under control.

Minutes later, chaos greeted them on the scene with bystanders, emergency vehicles and equipment spread out everywhere.

Royce did his own assessment as Felix brought the truck to a stop. The chief on the scene briefed Hershel since he was the captain of the company eight that would assist.

The older two-story brick house had an attic. Judging from the number of windows, there could be four or more bedrooms. One ladder was in position with a hose, flushing the flames. The fire had already burned a front first floor window, leaving a black streak racing upstairs.

An ambulance was nearby. EMS was administering oxygen to a woman and her teenage boy. Survivors—praise God. Thank God, there was some distance between the houses. Otherwise, the strong winds could have sparked adjacent fires.

His brother nodded to the lead commander and walked back to Royce, Felix and Allen.

"Four victims. The most serious have already been transported to Christian NE Hospital. Another one is en route to DePaul's. The good news—everyone is out. There is heavy damage in the front bedroom that had been occupied by an elderly man. The family says their uncle, who was on oxygen, was attempting to smoke in bed. Flames engulfed the room almost immediately."

Engine House Eight went to work. The blaze struck three alarms before the engine companies won the battle, dousing the flames from every angle possible.

To keep the fire from rekindling in hot spots, Royce and a fellow firefighter added foam to the water to cover spots that were still hot within the structure. Afterward, they scavenged through the structure to recover whatever valuables could be saved for the family.

When it appeared that the situation was under control, Royce began to wrap up the hoses as his mind returned to the red hot crossing guard. Why was the vision plaguing him when there was a strong possibility that she could be married?

Royce steered clear of women's advances if he knew they were married or had children. As far as he was concerned, life was too short to deal with drama. But the urge to find out if she was off limits was overpowering his common sense.

"Hey, Captain," Royce respected his brother's position when working together, "Mind if we go back by the way of Brandon's school?"

"Why?" he asked. When Royce stalled, Hershel wiped his brow. "Do I have to guess or are you going to tell me?"

"A woman with the nicest pair of legs…had my heart racing as if I downed a large double Espresso."

"What?" Hershel stared at him as if he had two heads, then snickered. "Was she washing cars or holding up a sign for Little Caesar's Pizza?"

"Actually, she was a crossing guard in front of Duncan Elementary."

Hershel's chuckle spiraled into a laugh. "A crossing guard," he mumbled as he nudged Royce toward the direction of the fire truck. "You're lusting after a crossing guard when you should've been praying, man."

"A man can multi-task, too, but a great pair of legs can distract any man."

Once they were back in the truck, Hershel looked over his shoulder at Royce and shook his head. Turning back to their chauffeur, he advised Felix to go past Duncan school.

"What? No Dunkin donuts? Oh man," he griped, steering the fire truck away from the curb as onlookers watched them. A few small children waved and Felix honked, acknowledging them. They cheered with their eyes wide with excitement.

Royce smiled. He loved children and he took his role as uncle to Hershel's two boys and his younger brother, Trent's daughter very seriously.

He wasn't surprised when their truck crawled to the stop light at the intersection where his mind had gone berserk—no crossing guard was in sight. School had been in session for more than an hour.

After stopping to get the donuts, they greeted their relief crew back at the station. While Hershel briefed the morning shift, Royce and the others headed to the showers and prepared to go home.

Royce believed in second chances. He knew in his heart he would see the lovely crossing guard again. He just prayed it wouldn't take another emergency call to cross paths.

Chapter 5

When Candace pulled into the company parking lot, Solae was milling outside the main entrance, talking with other coworkers. Once she spotted Candace, she left the group and headed her way.

"So how did it go?" Solae asked, opening her car door as if she was a valet. Her expression seemed hopeful for good news.

"Fine, except for almost getting hit by a fire truck." Candace shivered. She couldn't allow what happened to dredge up the memories of when her husband was struck and killed. She had to do this for Lindsay.

Her friend put a fist on her hip. "Would you stop exaggerating?" Rolling her eyes, she fell in step. "You survived."

"Barely." *Lord, You know how long it took me to even walk downtown near the intersection where Daniel died and I overcame that fear. Please don't let me develop one for fire trucks.*

"Every day will get better. You'll be delivered before you know it!"

How could she argue with that? Candace had no comeback.

"Well, you're here now, ready to start a new adventure in life," Solae said as they headed to the boss' office. There wasn't much paperwork to be done since she was already an employee—albeit a virtual one.

The day went by swiftly as Solae introduced Candace to one coworker after another. "It's nice to finally meet you in person," many of them said, welcoming her.

Candace wasn't too surprised to find that her small sleek half wall cubicle was angled perfectly across the aisle from Solae. It was stylish, cozy and just enough room for Lindsay should she have to bring her to work in the event Candace had to make up time. Thank God for a thirty-five hour work week and paid lunch, otherwise Lindsay may need a cot.

It was ironic that Candace had to come into the office to be considered for a promotion, but so many tasks were done via virtual assistant. Although it felt good to be away from her home office, she dearly missed hearing her daughter's chatter when Candace instructed her to be silent so she could get some work done.

The lunch break came without Candace realizing she was hungry. The cafeteria was massive with a dining room that boasted three sets of buffet bars: fruits, salads, soups, fried and baked entrees. After filling their trays with their selections, Solae chose a cozy spot in a far corner. Once they blessed their food, Solae tackled her salad. "Do you think you'll like it here?"

"Yep. It feels weird not to have Lindsay close by. I wonder if this is what empty-nesters feel like when their children grow up and move away. My baby is just in kindergarten."

Shaking her head, Candace enjoyed a mouthful of

chicken and wild rice soup. "Do you think I should get Lindsay a cell phone just in case she has an emergency?"

Solae almost choked. Reaching for her bottle of water, she took an unladylike swig. "You're kidding, right? If there is an emergency, the school will notify you. Girl, if you don't cut them strings and let Lindsay grow and explore her world, then I will unfriend you from Facebook."

Humph. Her best friend might be Lindsay's godmother, but Solae hadn't experienced the bond between mother and child. Wasn't worrying the norm?

Plus, Candace wasn't convinced that the world was all that safe to explore, especially after her husband was killed while simply walking across the street. No dangerous lifestyle, bad habits or health issues—just going from corner A to corner B.

Once lunch was over, Candace's first day breezed by quickly. She left work to fulfill her afternoon role as crossing guard. "Lord, will this get easier, or will I always be afraid? Help me, Jesus," she whispered as she got into her car and drove away. Surprisingly, the second shift was without incident—no more fire trucks—and she felt more in command. Candace felt like she was walking in victory as she strutted to her daughter's classroom to retrieve her and go home.

Lindsay was a ball of energy. "Mommy, my teacher let me collect the pencils today and tomorrow I'll..." Lindsay rambled on until they got home and continued as Candace prepared dinner.

She had never seen her daughter so happy. Lindsay talked non-stop about her teacher and what she learned in school and the many new friends.

Maybe being away from the little chatterbox during

the day wasn't such a bad idea after all. By week's end, Candace had settled into her positions as account executive assistant and crossing guard. She had to admit that her school duty was forcing her to face her fears, and in Jesus' name, overcome them. At her desk, snapshots of her and Lindsay littered her cubicle. She smiled at the pictorial timeline of her life with Lindsay

"Ouch!" Candace blinked. One thump on her head was followed by another one on her shoulder. Whirling around, she blocked her face with both hands from the peppermint ball attack. Candace was learning that it was Solae's choice of ammunition when she was trying to get her attention. "Stop it." She laughed. "What is your problem?"

"Well, I thought I was having a conversation with you until I realized you had zoned out on me and I was talking to myself." Solae scooted her chair out of her cubicle, across the carpet and rolled right into Candace's, bumping her chair.

"Now that you've got my attention, what do you want?"

Solae shrugged. "Actually, nothing. With the computers down and since I left my reading material at home, I thought I'd annoy you." She grinned and lifted a brow. "So are you getting the hang of standing on the corner?"

"Funny." Candace stuck out her tongue. "Some of the older children want me to dance in the street like Chris Rock in that *Rush Hour* movie or wear white gloves like a clown or blow a whistle like I was in a marching band." She chuckled. "For some reason, they think it's cool."

"Or use those legs like a majorette. That's all these brothers have been talking about since you walked into this office."

"I'm not interested in romance in or out of the office. I have a little one to fill my life. I don't have time for a man." Candace reached for her bottle of water to take a sip.

"Well, Lindsay is going to need a daddy, and I think this is a good time for us to start looking for the right material."

Candace accidentally sprayed Solae with the water she was sipping. "Us?"

"I mean you," Solae corrected, pointing.

"I thought you were throwing your hat in the ring, too." Candace eyed her friend until they both started to giggle. Once she sobered, Candace cleared her throat. "I had a good man and I doubt there is another one out there."

"Daniel was a good man and husband, but he never got the chance to be that good father to Lindsay. She's going to need a daddy in her life, so you might want to pray on it." With that said she rolled her chair back to her desk.

Uh-uh, Solae was not going to have the last word on that. "I don't have to pray on it. The Bible says he who finds a wife finds a good thing. If Lindsay's substitute daddy is out there," she paused and patted her chest. "Let him find me. That is all."

Royce's week ended without another sighting of the mystery crossing guard. He even compromised a much-needed late morning sleep-in by setting his alarm clock, so he could be at the intersection early enough to meet her.

That scheme didn't work. With his body feeling like

lead, Royce slept right through the siren sound effect alarm on his phone. Running out of options, Royce hinted to Hershel that maybe Brandon could ask around for him.

Hershel didn't crack a smile. "See you this weekend at Trent and Julia's house. Don't even think about bribing my son then."

The weekend meant their sister-in-law would whip up a home cooked meal for them. With both parents deceased, the brothers were determined to maintain a tight family bond.

On Saturday, Royce slept throughout the day until his stomach roared. Getting up, he showered and dressed, then showed up at their doorstep hungry. "What's up, bro?" Trent answered with his six-month-old daughter, Ariel, in his arms.

His niece smiled at him. Royce peppered her neck with kisses and was rewarded with a taunting laugh for him to do it again.

In no time the table was set with stir-fry vegetables, smothered pork chops, garlic potatoes, tossed salad, rolls, and banana pudding holding in the refrigerator. Trent, the first brother in the family to repent of his sins and be baptized in Jesus' name—in part because he wanted Julia, who was already a practicing Christian—did the honors of saying grace.

"Lord, in the name of Jesus, we thank You for this food. We ask that You sanctify it from all impurities and bless it. I also thank You for protecting my brothers as they serve others and continue to bless them, God, in Jesus' name. Amen."

"Amen," Royce murmured, touched by his brother's prayer. Younger by three years, Trent wasn't a public servant, but was a certified public accountant.

Julia added, "And find him a wife."

She shrugged when Royce looked at her. With an angelic expression to match that of her daughter, she slipped a spoonful of mashed potatoes in her mouth.

"Maybe she's a crossing guard," Trent snickered. "Sorry, man." His grin conveyed anything but repentance. "Hershel said it was too good not to tell."

Snarling, Royce would have a word with his brother later. "It's a simple curiosity about a good-looking lady. Our brother won't even let my nephew snoop around for me.

"If I only had a kid to walk to school, it would be a decoy to learn more about her."

"You might start with a baby first, or I can loan you mine. Women love babies," Julia said and she spooned a serving of baby spinach in her daughter's mouth. His niece ate everything—table food, baby food and would wash it down with a bottle of milk.

Borrow? "Why didn't I think of that? Thanks, Julia. One day tops." Royce was already formulating a plan.

"I was just kidding," Julia continued to bring him back to reality. "Besides, she's probably married or somebody's mother. If you're ready to pursue that special someone, let me introduce you to someone."

He had to satisfy his curiosity about the crossing guard first. "I'll let you know when," was his standard reply when she offered her free matchmaking services. Once dinner was finished, Trent helped Julia clean the kitchen.

Assigned to babysitting duties, Royce cradled Ariel in his arms until she dozed off.

His nephews, five-year-old Brandon and his three-year-old brother, Harrison, played one of the many games

31

Trent and Julia kept for them when they visited.

Hershel nudged him when he yawned. "Go home, dude, so you can get some sleep."

"Yeah, you're right." Normally, his long shifts didn't wear him out so much on his off days, but with some of the twenty-hour shifts lately thrown in the mix, Royce's body was protesting. Ariel stirred in his arms as he shifted his weight.

As if on cue, Trent reappeared and took his sleeping baby. Saying his goodbyes, Royce received hugs and then headed to the door.

"We'll see you at church in the morning," Julia said.

"Yep." Whenever he had a Sunday off, which could be a few times a month, Royce strove to be in morning service. With his keys jingling in his hand, he got into his car and drove off. At home, he showered, then crashed without setting his alarm.

The next morning, Royce woke drowsy an hour later than he wanted. He rushed through a shave, dressed and microwaved a frozen breakfast meal. He ate it in record time. He might be late for worship service at Rapture Ready Church, but he would probably still beat Hershel there.

Years earlier, Hershel's ex-wife had attended the same church and listened to the same message, but that didn't stop her from cheating on Hershel. Eventually, she left him and abandoned their two small sons.

Although his faith in God and women were shaken, Hershel came on most of his off days, usually blaming his tardiness on the boys. Sometimes Royce wondered if Hershel's attendance was for an example to his sons, going through the motions, or believing God despite what his ex-wife did to shake his faith.

Royce slid into the pew next to Trent and his family. He knelt and said a quick prayer of thanks for being in the house of the Lord. Within minutes, the praise and worship segment began. The harmony and repetitious words of the chorus always seemed to clear his head of the tragedies and hardships from the previous week.

Hershel and the boys arrived five minutes into it. The pastor's sermon: The power of God's presence in our lives.

"We live in a spiritual realm. God just might be trying to get your attention…If we connect the dots of events that happen in our lives or people we meet, we'll find out that Jesus was in the mix all the time to draw us closer to Him and His purpose…" Pastor Reed admonished his congregation.

"Pay attention to the things that you would normally brush off as unimportant…" he finished less than an hour later. During the altar call, five souls repented and requested the baptism in Jesus' name to wash their sins away. The applause was thunderous. Rapture Ready Church members believed in rejoicing with each soul that was snatched away from Satan's grip.

Chapter 6

What anxiety? Candace taunted at the devil. Every day she was getting stronger in her faith as the fear lessened of crossing the street.

What mattered most was the children's safe passage to school. Some days it was a challenge with the free-spirited skate boarders and bicyclists.

She had even begun to match students' names with their faces, like now as she peered over her shoulder down a side street. "Tommy, slow down," she fussed at a fourth grader who seemed bent on racing a fellow classmate to the corner.

Turning back, Candace's hand hovered over the pedestrian crossing button. Before she could activate the walk signal, a driver slammed on his brakes at the same time Tommy sped past her and his bike made contact with the car's front bumper. She reacted in slow motion; the scream was lodged in Candace's throat, but the children yelled.

Oh my God. Oh Lord. Not again. Her heart pounded, then she remembered the children, including Lindsay. Forcing back her fears, Candace instructed the students to look away and not to move.

Waving the stop sign in the air, she raced to the boy who had slid off the hood of the car to the ground. "Tommy, are you okay?"

Tommy moaned as he tried to open his eyes. "My leg hurts, Lindsay's mommy. It hurts. Ooh."

The driver jumped out the car. "I didn't see him," he pleaded. The man was just as frantic as she would be if she were in the same situation. "He came out of nowhere."

Candace could only nod her understanding as she dialed 9-1-1 from her iPhone strapped to her waist. The sirens wailing in the background provided her little comfort if Tommy injuries were more serious than what she could see.

"9-1-1. What's your emergency?" the dispatcher answered.

Taking a breath to calm her nerves, Candace stuttered, "I have….struck. A child, a boy…he's been hit at the intersection of Lindbergh and Cougar in front of the Duncan Elementary School. Yes, he is conscious and breathing. Hurry," she pleaded as the woman had her repeat what she just tried to say.

Traffic had come to a stop on its own. The children remained at the corner. Horror was stretched across their faces as they looked on. Several encircled the boy.

"I'm a doctor," a gray-haired man said as he bent to assess Tommy's vitals.

"It's going to be okay, son." He asked a series of questions, which the child answered through his tears.

"Miss Clark, do you need any help?" A parent came to her aid.

"Yes, will you escort these children to their classes and notify Mrs. Lovejoy what happened so the teachers can talk to their students."

Lord, I know I didn't want this job, but You know I don't want to be relieved of my duties because I was negligent.

The parent patted her on the shoulder and went to tend to the other children as a fire truck arrived behind an ambulance. A paramedic rushed to Tommy and began to stabilize him.

"What happened?" the EMT asked of no one in particular, but the driver was the first to respond as Tommy grabbed her hand and held on.

"I was driving at the speed limit. I had a green light and this boy came from out of nowhere…"

A female officer took charge of directing traffic so the new group of students at the corner could be escorted safely across the street.

Another EMT assisted the first man with securing a brace around Tommy's neck and support under both legs before lifting him onto a stretcher.

As the child began to cry in earnest, Candace tried to coax his mother's number from him so she could call her.

After three attempts, the boy finally recited all seven digits. Candace's hand shook as she punched in the number. She empathized with any bearer of bad news. Candace swallowed as the phone rang. She had to remain calm as a woman answered.

"Mrs. Harris, this is Miss Clark, the crossing guard at your son's school." Her lips froze as she relived the moment when she was on the other end of the phone, hearing the officer's words that her husband was dead.

Closing her eyes, Candace slowly forced out the words, "There has been an accident with Tommy and his bike."

"Oh my God. Is he…alive?" Mrs. Harris's piercing scream of terror made Candace shivered.

"Yes, yes. He's just complaining about pain in his leg. The ambulance is here…"

Mrs. Harris disconnected without another word. Getting off her knees, Candace exhaled. A crowd lined the sidewalk.

As she pressed her way through the crowd, Candace couldn't get the images out her mind: Daniel and Tommy.

She had to sit down before her legs gave way. With her car within sight, she took one step after the other as the what-ifs began to overwhelm her. Could she have stopped Tommy?

Should she have turned around so soon? Should she have even taken the assignment?

She had almost made it to her Kia when she felt light-headed and her legs—like Jell-O—began to melt, then her vision blurred before everything went black.

Royce couldn't believe it. A child struck in front of his nephew's school had brought him face-to-face with the crossing guard who had dominated his thoughts since day one.

From her flushed face, he could tell she was in shock. The child's mother came running down to the scene as if the wind propelled her, then heaved her body into the ambulance before they shut the door.

With one situation under control, Royce shamelessly checked the crossing guard's ring finger—nothing.

Under the pretense of asking if she needed medical attention, he followed her. Only to catch her before she collapsed. Evidently, the scene was too much for her.

Responding to medical emergencies was part of his job. Evidently, this woman had experienced a horrific scene like this before, possibly involving a child.

"Is she okay?" Felix asked over his shoulder as Royce checked her pulse.

Royce nodded and began to speak to her while Felix put an oxygen mask over her face. The woman's lids fluttered as she struggled to open her eyes.

When she succeeded, he noticed they were a beautiful shade of brown.

Officer Williams walked over and squatted. "Was she injured? I need to get her statement."

At that moment, the woman stirred.

"Give her a few minutes. She's probably in shock," Felix told the officer.

"Hey, easy there. I've got you. Are you okay?"

She nodded before she drifted away again.

"Let's get her in an ambulance, so she can be checked out," Hershel ordered as he quickly assessed the situation. Operating in his captain capacity, his brother was clueless that this was the crossing guard who'd snagged his attention.

As Hershel summoned the paramedics to tend to the crossing guard, it took all within Royce to release her. But his brother was the captain and Royce had to follow orders.

The firefighters were climbing in the truck as the second ambulance, carrying the woman, pulled away. Royce prayed that she was okay. Twice, the crossing guard had snagged his attention. However, her falling into his arms was not the introduction he had expected.

Chapter 7

Candace opened her eyes and was immediately disoriented by her surroundings. Then it dawned on her that she was in the emergency room.

Instantly, it clicked what happened at the crosswalk. She blinked, staring into Solae's worried expression.

"Tommy…is Tommy okay?"

"Yes." Solae put pressure on her chest to keep her from getting up.

"He's fine—and alive with a broken leg. His mother just left from checking on you. The doctors say it could have been worse."

"How embarrassing." Candace groaned as she eyed the machines monitoring her heart and blood pressure. Turning her head away, she began to cry. "God, will I ever overcome this? I had no business…"

"Stop it, Candace Clark! There was nothing anybody could have done to avoid it, except Tommy and we know children think the world revolves around them. I am not the one for a pity party today." Solae lowered her voice. "Don't take on burdens that aren't yours. God knew this was going to happen. Tommy learned a lesson and I believe Jesus is teaching you one."

Candace sniffed as Solae embraced her in a consoling hug.

"Stop torturing yourself," she whispered. "Daniel was a baptized believer. He died in Christ and will rise with Him in the rapture. Your late husband is resting until that trumpet sounds, so he's okay. I know Daniel would want you to be okay, too."

God always gave Solae words of wisdom beyond her years when Candace needed them. "You're right. No invites to a pity party." Candace mustered up a smile.

Sitting on the bed, Solae closed her eyes and began to pray. "Jesus, my sister needs You. Lord, mend her heart. Give her the victory over fear, in Jesus' name. Amen."

"And shut the devil out," they said in unison whenever they prayed together.

Opening their eyes, they smiled as the doctor walked into the room. "Miss Clark, your EKG came back fine and so did your blood work. I think you just experienced shock. I suggest you go home and get some rest."

Half an hour later, Candace was discharged and Solae drove her home.

"What about my car? I need to get Lindsay and call about a replacement for a crossing guard. I'm sure I'm fired now."

"I will get Lindsay, call the principal and take you to get your car in the morning. You've had enough excitement for one day."

Candace didn't argue as she closed her eyes and lay back on the headrest. *Thank God for girlfriends.* Solae was irreplaceable.

Once they were at her two bedroom bungalow, Solae made sure she got under the covers, then called the school and spoke with the principal. Since she was already on the list, there wouldn't be a problem with her picking up Lindsay.

"Mrs. Lovejoy said to get your rest, and she'll do the crossing guard duties this afternoon."

Candace burst out laughing.

"What's so funny?" Solae chuckled along.

Laughing felt good after the morning she'd had, so Candace let her amusement run its course while holding her stomach. "Mrs. Lovejoy is barely taller than some of the middle school students. You think we can do a drive by this afternoon so I can watch her try and stop traffic?"

"Absolutely not!" Solae waggled her finger and then kissed her cheek before leaving.

Candace closed her eyes and snuggled under her cover. She giggled, thinking about Mrs. Lovejoy doing a job she was bent on Candace doing.

A merry heart doeth good like a medicine: but a broken spirit dries the bones, the Lord whispered Proverbs 17:22. My joy comes in the morning.

"Thank You, Lord," Candace mumbled as she drifted off to sleep with a smile.

"Mommy, you're coming to my class this morning, right?" Lindsay asked as Candace ushered her out the house.

Opening the car door, Candace frowned as Lindsay climbed into the back, then proudly clicked her belt on the booster seat herself.

"Why, sweetie?" she asked double-checking it.

"Mommies and daddies are coming and tell us about their jobs."

Candace chuckled. "Oh, honey, there is nothing exciting about Mommy's job." She sat behind the wheel and adjusted the mirror. *Your daddy had an exciting job— product designer. That man had a talent for sketching. Of course, there's no sense in bringing that up. Daniel is gone.*

"But you stop the cars, so you're the boss. My friends say you're nice and pretty..."

There had been one car she couldn't stop. It had been more than a week since Tommy's accident. When the images attempted to replay in Candace's mind, she rebuked them and shut the devil out. Candace thought the school might remove her from her position. Under any other circumstances Candace would have rejoiced, but Mrs. Lovejoy assured her no one faulted her for Tommy's horseplay that resulted in his broken leg.

Lindsay continued to rattle on as she bounced from topic to topic for almost the entire drive. "Okay, Mommy?"

"Hmm-mm," Half-listening, Candace answered absentmindedly. Minutes later, she pulled into a vacant space and parked.

"Yay!" Lindsay clapped her hands. She displayed a missing tooth smile and she unfastened her belt once Candace opened the back door.

Keeping her daughter at her side, she retrieved her stop sign and vest from the trunk.

"Yay what, young lady?" She laughed as she lifted her daughter's backpack off the seat. Holding onto Lindsay's arm, Candace watched her daughter leap off the inside edge of the car to the ground.

"You're coming to my class."

"Baby, I've already explained to you that my job isn't something I can show and tell. I don't wear a uniform or anything," she said, slipping on her red vest. Plus, how much of a positive role model could she be after what happened?

"But Mommy, your stop sign is a uniform because it helps you do your job. You said you were coming." Lindsay's pouty lips worked every time.

"I'll come, but as soon as I do my presentation I have to get to work. Okay, young lady?" She squatted to be eye level with her, thinking about the time she would have to makeup.

Lindsay bobbed her head. Candace lifted a brow, letting her daughter know that was not an acceptable form of communication. "Yes, ma'am."

"Good." Taking a deep breath, Candace walked to the light. Lindsay skipped alongside her. With more diligence and prayer, she refused to have a repeat of another accident on her watch.

Royce moaned at the annoying noise as he rolled over in his bed. If it wasn't the shriek of an emergency alarm, he wasn't budging.

When the irritating sound of his phone ceased, Royce grinned without opening one eye, then snuggled deeper into his pillow. He couldn't resist the fresh scent of his fabric softener.

Surrendering to the lull of a deep sleep, Royce relaxed

at the same moment his cell phone rang. The theme to Superman chime jolted him awake, identifying the caller. What did Hershel want?

Snarling, Royce reached across the bed for his cell phone on the night stand. It fell on the carpet. He fumbled for it. When he had it within his grip, he barked into the phone, "In case you forgot, this is my day off. O-F-F….unless the engine station is on fire literally…"

"I know. I'm really sorry, but I need a big favor."

Royce's eyelids fluttered closed. Drifting, he slurred, "Sorry, they're on backorder."

"Listen, bro, I need a favor. I'm still at work. We had a long night in Jefferson County with a meth lab, but listen. Today is Career Day at Brandon's school. You know my boy. He's been bragging about fire prevention. Do me a favor and play firefighter and go wow the kids for me."

"Isn't that what the firefighters "on duty" do as part of their community awareness, not the off duty firefighter who needs rest and was in the middle of a dream and…" he mumbled.

"You must be brain sleep. You've been pining over that crossing guard for more than a week."

"Correction, I've been praying for her. I was just concerned," he defended.

"Earth to Royce. You might catch her if you go to the school…"

Finally putting two and two together, Royce sprang up in bed instantly alert. "I can't disappoint my nephew." He glanced at the clock as he tussled with his covers. "Okay."

He leaped out of bed as if he was about to respond to a four-alarm fire. "Bye." Racing into his bathroom, Royce blinked at his reflection in the mirror. "Great." He needed a shave, but it wasn't happening that morning if he was going to get to Duncan School in time to see the crossing guard.

Once Royce showered, then hurried to his basement, hoping and praying that he had some leftover safety packets for handouts. Although the firefighting gear was at the station, Royce had an old helmet and jacket. He would have to forgo the boots. Grabbing everything within reach, he made the trip to his car.

His heart pounded with anticipation. He was almost at Duncan Elementary school when sirens from EMS forced him to momentarily pull over. When he arrived, the crossing guard and children were nowhere in sight.

Chapter 8

Once Candace located a spot in the school's main parking lot, she called her boss and explained the last minute surprise.

"That's not a problem, as long as you make up the missed time," her supervisor, Mr. Hawkins said.

Anticipating his response, Candace had already worked out an option. "I know we're backlogged with follow-up calls. If I can bring Lindsay back to work with me this afternoon, I can make it up today. I can also send her home with Solae."

"That's doable. As you know, we are a family friendly business. Do whatever you need to do, so long as neither home, nor work suffers," he advised.

"Yes sir." Candace nodded as if her supervisor could see her, thanking him. She checked her watch. Career Day had already started.

She silently prayed that the children wouldn't think she was a fraud because of what happened.

With a sigh, Candace stepped out of her car and smoothed out the wrinkles in her simple jade colored dress and reached for her stop sign.

As she stretched across the seat, she heard a rip and it didn't come from her undersized underwear—it was her new pair of pantyhose.

"Great, a run." She gritted her teeth in frustration. How awkward would it be to stand in front of a class of children and other professionals with a hole, resembling a spider's web that stretched with each movement? She checked both legs—nothing yet. Hopefully, it would stay at its position until she finished her presentation.

Carefully walking, Candace entered the building and stopped at the school office to sign in and get a guest badge for Career Day. Mrs. Lovejoy waved. She continued to measure her stride down the hall to Lindsay's classroom.

She felt foolish breezing into a classroom in a worn safety vest and carrying a stop sign as if she had invented it, like African-American inventor Garrett Morgan with the traffic light.

Outside Mrs. Davis' kindergarten room, Candace peeped inside. Lindsay's teacher was already making introductions as she quietly opened the door.

"Excellent. I see another parent has arrived." The teacher clasped her hands in appreciation. "Lindsay would you like to introduce your mother?"

Lindsay bobbed her head and stood. "My Mommy is the best crossing guard in the whole world," she said proudly and retook her seat.

Candace's heart warmed. Her daughter would always be her number one fan. She glanced at the other participants.

There was a nurse, wearing a white wingtip hat and a man in scrubs represented the medical field. Another woman held colorful ballet shoes in her hands—probably a dancer or instructor. At the end of the line was a firefighter.

She shivered under his gaze. He looked somewhat familiar, but she had never met him. Self-consciously, she wondered if he was making fun of her "profession".

Despite his scrutiny of her, she had to pull her eyes away from him. Bulging muscles outlined his polo uniform shirt. Candace had never seen such a handsome man, even more so than her husband Daniel, and he was good-looking.

Re-directing her attention to the man in the scrubs who happened to be an anesthesiologist, Candace couldn't shake the feeling that the firefighter was still watching her.

"It's very important that I monitor the mixture of medication so that the heart beat…"

Although Dr. Whitman's career was impressive, the children seemed to have blank expressions. Even the man's son appeared bored. Candace barely understood some of the terms he rattled off and she had an undergraduate degree in liberal arts from Fontbonne University in St. Louis.

That's why the new position at Kendall Printing was important. With a promotion she would actually be using her marketing degree to grow her income.

Mrs. Davis gave the doctor a signal that his time was up. Everyone, including the teacher, sighed in relief before she encouraged her class to clap. Candace was surprised that the teacher gestured for her to go next.

Already? Clearing her throat, Candace took baby steps, mindful of her run, to be front and center of the students. She relaxed as several children waved at her. Smiling, she waved back, warmed by their acceptance.

"Good morning, class. Many of you already know me. I'm Miss Clark, Lindsay's mother."

One girl in the back raised her hand. "You help us cross the street every day."

"Yes, I do." Candace nodded. "Besides looking both ways, always make sure you're standing at a corner. After you push the button to walk, wait until all cars and trucks stop before stepping off the curb."

She briefly thought about her husband. If only he had followed protocol and waited. The driver never slowed down, even after hitting Daniel, then dragging him for several feet. Candace definitely didn't want to scare them with those details. Many bystanders had witnessed Tommy's accident.

"You have a stop sign, Mommy. You can make the cars stop." Lindsay added when Candace's mind played the flashback.

"Children, wait until each guest is finished before you ask any questions," Mrs. Davis kindly reminded the class although it was only her daughter who had violated the rule.

"Thank you," Candace whispered and then continued. "The street can be a scary place..."

"Tommy got hurt," that statement came from a student in the back.

Candace took a deep breath. Although she didn't want to take the blame, she didn't want to put it on Tommy, either. "Thank God Tommy is okay. That's why you never play in the streets or near them. Always wait for your crossing guard to give you the signal when it's safe to cross."

She did her best to give helpful hints, considering she didn't prepare anything. Candace finished and more hands flew up.

"How do you get the sign to flash?" a boy in the front row asked seriously.

49

Another child followed up. "Can you dance?"

"Yes, but not in the streets." *Dancing.* She hadn't been dancing since she and Daniel celebrated confirmation of her pregnancy.

"Chris Tucker did in a movie…" The boy grinned, describing in detail the movie *Rush Hour II.* It was amazing how much their young minds absorbed the wrong things.

"But the drivers crashed their cars, right?" She reiterated, "People can get hurt playing in the street. My job is to make sure you stay safe. You can help me if you follow the rules." Candace momentarily felt like the teacher.

Mrs. Davis stepped in and rescued Candace. "Let's thank our wonderful speaker."

To her amazement, she received thunderous applause. Humbled, Candace turned to leave when Lindsay jumped up and rewarded her with a hug. When she squatted to receive it, she felt the run stretch down her leg. *Oh no. At least I'm done.*

"Thank you, Mommy," she whispered loudly.

Tapping the tip of her nose, Candace smiled. Her daughter's happiness meant everything to her. Standing slowly, Candace inched her way to the door, stepping backwards. She experienced a chill again that she was being watched by someone other than the students.

Glancing at the remaining speakers, sure enough, it was the firefighter who Mrs. Davis motioned to next.

Ignoring the teacher, his attention left her face and traveled down to her legs. She inwardly groaned. *That's it.* Feeling self-conscious, Candace whirled around and hurried out the classroom. Next stop—a beauty supply store to stock up on enough nylons for a month.

Miss Clark. She looked just as beautiful as the day he held her in his arms. Worried about her fate, Royce had made intercessory prayers on her behalf. Thank God, she seemed fine and glowed when she smiled.

Her full lips got to him. Although he wanted to kiss them, Royce would have to settle for kissing Hershel—on the forehead or something—for orchestrating another chance meeting with the crossing guard. From the moment she walked in the classroom, Royce was captivated.

He performed another ring check as she identified herself as "Miss". Whether she was divorced or never married, Royce would have to adjust his self-imposed restriction of no children in a relationship, because Lindsay was a cutie pie.

Still, he took the absence of a ring as a go ahead to ogle her. Even in that over-sized red vest, there was no question of her figure. Her brown hair brushed her shoulders.

The greenish-blue dress complemented her caramel skin tone. Suddenly, it became his favorite color. And the hem teased her knees, allowing him to appreciate how God had formed each limb of her body. He smirked at that run in her stockings. It did nothing to distract from the allure of her legs and how fast she used them to escape his scrutiny.

"He's my uncle and the best firefighter besides my dad, who you have to call captain." Brandon added that tidbit as he proudly introduced him, causing Royce to rein in his thoughts.

Although Royce winked at his nephew, his mind reverted back to Miss Clark on its own accord. He tapped into his autopilot mode and recited info he could mumble in his sleep. "Firefighters are your friends, but a fire is not. Don't be afraid and hide when you see us in our mask. We are there to rescue you. Never try to put a fire out. Yell to warn others to get out. If you see smoke, call 9-1-1. Don't try to take things with you like your favorite toy. Get out quickly. Your house could be burning before you can count to one hundred…"

He wrapped up his spiel minutes later and passed out packets that included decals for each child's bedroom window. "Remember, when the smoke goes up…" he cupped his ear.

"We drop down so we can breathe," the class shouted back at him.

Satisfied, Royce nodded. As the students clapped, he waved and strolled out of the classroom. Immediately, his mind returned to the crossing guard. It took pure restraint for Royce not to follow her out the class and engage her in a private conversation. But it was all good; Royce had a name, a face, a ring-less finger and a great pair of legs to occupy his thoughts.

Chapter 9

Thirty minutes later, Candace was dumping the contents of her plastic shopping bag on her desk when Solae strolled into her cubicle.

"So what did you talk about? How to strut across the street in stilettoes..." Solae joked, then frowned. "Ah, what's with the stockpile of pantyhose?"

"I had a run." Candace didn't offer details as she removed her lightweight jacket and twirled it onto the back of her chair. When she thought about the run, the firefighter's face and the intense way he looked at her flashed before her eyes.

If he hadn't been so handsome, the uneasiness he caused her would have been creepy. But it was as if he was spellbound.

"I changed in the restroom before I came to my desk." Candace answered the question before Solae could ask as she scrutinized Candace's stockings.

"Okay..." Solae stole Candace's seat and began counting the Ultra-sheen stocking packages that she purchased at a neighborhood Korean beauty supply store. "And you needed ten pair to replace one run? How big was

53

it, the size of your whole leg?"

"I'll never leave home without an extra pair in my purse again. Call it ammunition."

Sitting on the edge of her desk, Candace shook her head. "I have never felt so self-conscious before in my life. Well, except for the emergency room trip because I freaked out. All I could think about was Daniel."

"Since you're still struggling with that, let's start back with our morning prayers. Get up fifteen minutes early. It is so past time to shut the devil down on this once and for all," Solae scolded her, then folded her arms. "Now, changing the subject. You should be a pro as a crossing guard by now, so how could a bunch of kindergarteners intimidate you?"

"Girl, it wasn't the children. They were so cute with their questions, and only one boy broke up the…you know what," Candace snuck that in there before leaning forward and lowering her voice, "It was one of the parents. I felt he—"

"He?" Solae lifted her brows. "Hmm, tell me more."

Solae's hopeful expression amused her. Candace thought about letting her friend stew, then decided against teasing her.

"It was something about his smothering eyes that made me feel like a little rag doll with my raggedy stockings."

"Humph." Solae *tsk*ed. I guarantee you that man was admiring your legs, run and all, so how did he look?" Anchoring her elbow on Candace's desk, Solae rested her chin in the cup of her hand, seemingly waiting for a long story.

"Very good-looking man." Standing, Candace slid her

purchases in her drawer, then moved her mouse so her computer screen would come to life, giving Candace the hint she had work to do and was already late getting to it.

Plus, if she admitted that he sparked her attraction, Solae would probably faint. That would be a first since Daniel's death.

"That's it?" Her friend feigned insult.

"Yep, now I have clients to call. Do you mind?"

Squinting, Solae was slow to vacate her chair. When she did, Candace gave her a few more nuggets. "If I didn't already have a hole in my nylons, then his smoldering eyes would have burned a hole in them like Superman."

"Ooh." Her friend's eyes danced with excitement. "Remember Sunday's sermon that all things work together for the good to those who love the Lord?"

"Yes, but I can't see how Romans 8:28 applies to me and a hole. That sure wasn't a good thing or of any spiritual significance," Candace argued.

"Don't be so sure. I believe God uses insignificant to get our attention. Maybe the run in your stockings caused Mr. Firefighter's interest to pique."

"Boy, you're really trying to make that scripture work for you. Hang it up." Candace shook her head as she typed in her username and password.

Indignant to the core, Solae planted a fist on her hip. "It's not impossible. When men look at you, you have to think interest. I told you, you're too young to hang up your dating hat. You're pretty, in shape and have nice legs, judging from the whispers I've heard around here since the day you started coming to the office. I think if you strut in here with a pair of pants on, the men in the office would be in an uproar."

Solae needed to look in the mirror. She always had been the prettier one between them. With exotic features that favored a well-known actress and former Junior Miss runner-up, her friend was the one who would and could catch a man's eye. But keeping his heart was tricky once he learned that her baby factory equipment had been removed.

"Maybe he's a single parent, too. You should find out—"

"I'll date when Lindsay gets older. I'm still adjusting to our long hours of separation."

"Cut the cord." She made a snipping gesture with her fingers. "Make sure it's not when my godchild is about to become a grandmother." She turned around to head back to her cubicle and almost bumped into a coworker, sipping on a cup of coffee. "Oh, I'm sorry."

"No, it was me who wasn't looking where I was going." Her tall bald dark-skinned admirer's husky voice practically cooed his apology. Judging by that expression, he would forgive her for anything.

What about not having children? Candace wondered. At least she had somebody—Lindsay. Maybe the real matchmaking should be finding a mate for Solae. With the attention off of her, Candace pulled up the accounts that she was scheduled to call.

Sometime later, a peppermint bounced off her shoulder. Knowing the culprit, Candace sighed as she twirled around. Angling her body, she eyed Solae. "Girl, you've been doing that since the day I came in the office. Are you trying to tell me I've got bad breath?"

"Nope, I've been thinking—"

"Always a cause for concern." Candace grinned.

"Funny. It might be time for you to pucker up the

56

next time you see that firefighter."

"Really? Are you back on that again?" Candace picked up her phone to resume her client calls. She was not about to get drawn into another dating conversation with her friend that day. Solae seemed to have other plans, but the client picked the right time to answer her call.

"Jake Greenlee."

The longtime customer of Kendall Printing seemed grateful for the follow up call, but wasn't convinced that her branding proposal was worth the added expense.

Before ending the conversation, Candace finally persuaded Mr. Greenlee to meet with an account executive. She needed as many appointments as possible for her to shadow as part of the prerequisite to her training program.

Soon it was time for Candace to leave for her crossing guard duty. "I'll be back with Lindsay in a few hours. It'll be like old times when I used to work at home and she was close by. She was quiet then. Now, she's a little chatterbox…of course, you can always volunteer to take her home. Hint, hint."

"Girl, please. I'll take my god-baby, feed her and make sure she does her homework, so when you come and get Lindsay, she'll be ready for her bath and bed."

"Thank you."

Back at her post while she waited on her first wave of students at the crosswalk, Candace dared to think about the firefighter. Whose father was he? Was he a single parent like her? Suddenly, Candace wrinkled her nose. If the jerk was married, his wife should smack him for ogling her.

Chapter 10

nd we know that all things work together for good to them that love God, to them who are the called according to his purpose. For some unknown reason, Romans 8:28 stayed with Royce after he finished reading the chapter. Was God going to reveal a nugget of wisdom? Nothing came.

Closing his Bible, he walked into the kitchen to warm up leftovers when a vision of the breathtaking Miss Clark beckoned to him. The woman had been in and out of his mind all day since leaving the classroom earlier.

Of course, Royce wasn't complaining as he entertained the vision, which always brought him to the query as to why she was *Miss* Clark instead of *Mrs*. He could only think of two reasons: divorced or single with a child.

His phone rang as he popped his plate in the microwave. He programmed three minutes as noted Hershel's name on the caller ID.

"I'm giving you a heads up that our dear sister-in-law convinced me that I should let her plan Brandon's birthday party. I told her to go for it, so everything is set for next Saturday at Terrence's Ranch. She assigned you to help supervise."

His nephews' parties were legendary. When it came to his sons, Hershel went overboard. His reasoning was that bigger was better to justify inviting what seemed like an entire city to celebrate the boys' birthdays ever since they were toddlers. It was his way to make up for the absence of their mother.

"Bro, did you forget *you* scheduled me to work a twenty-hour shift that happens to end that morning?"

"Hey, blame it on Julia who decided to schedule the party for next Saturday since Brandon's birthday is in the middle of the week."

If it wasn't for the fact that he only had two nephews, Royce would skip it. "I'll be at Terrence's in time for cleanup."

"Brandon wants to invite the whole class—all twenty-one rug rats," Hershel casually mentioned.

"And your point is?" Royce took his plate out of the microwave the minute it beeped. Taking it to the table, he took his seat. "Hold on."

Royce silently said grace and then dug into the baked chicken, corn on the cob, and baked beans.

"*Hello*. Did you not stop by the engine house this morning— on your day off, mind you—to inform me that the same crossing guard who collapsed in your arms was one of the speakers? Did you not hug me because I asked you nicely to fill in for me?" He chuckled. "Royce, I'm inviting Brandon's *entire class*."

The realization sunk in. Miss Clark might bring her daughter. Royce swallowed his food. "You know, I'd do anything for my favorite nephew. What time do you want me there?"

After Hershel recovered from a hearty laugh, he gave Royce the details.

"Lindsay got another invite in the mail yesterday," Candace mentioned casually as she and Solae lunched at Applebee's across the street from their workplace.

Sipping on her lemonade, Solae grinned. "Those things are coming like junk mail."

"Who you tellin'? I guess Lindsay and I will be shopping after work. I'm becoming a social butterfly without trying," Candace joked.

"You know I love you, but there has to be more to your life than crashing kindergarteners' birthday parties. What does this make, two weekends in a row?"

"Three. I think half the children in the class are September babies. Thank God Lindsay's birthday is in the summer."

Solae seemed thoughtful as she glanced out the window. "It's been a while since we've had some us time. Why don't we go to the movies for a few hours?"

"I took Lindsay to the matinees last—"

"See… that's what I'm talking about, girl. Will you cut the string? Okay, let's go shopping…and you're forbidden from buying Lindsay another thing." She pointed a manicured finger at her.

Candace didn't back down as she tried to make her friend understand. "Now that she's in school all day and I'm working outside the home, the weekends are all I have with her. She's all I have." *All I have of Daniel,* Candace didn't voice.

"As your friend, sister and Lindsay's godmother, you either go with me and we do something fun for a change, so that my god-baby has room to grow, or I'm crashing this party. I mean it."

Candace rolled her eyes at Solae's theatrics. "All right, all right, but I'll need to stay at least five minutes to chat with the parents and check out the place for safety hazards. The invitation says pony rides and a petting zoo."

Beaming, Solae lifted her arms in the air as if she had scored a touchdown. "Yes! Well, wouldn't you say this was a productive lunch? It looks like the negotiations went well."

Balling up a napkin, Candace aimed it at her and fired. Solae ducked, but not soon enough. They cleared the table and headed back to work, laughing.

Chapter 11

Saturday morning, Lindsay couldn't contain her excitement about riding a baby horse at Brandon Kavanaugh's party. Candace dressed her in a denim jumpsuit and cowgirl boots.

She even loosely tied a red bandana around Lindsay's neck and twisted her thick hair into two ponytails.

Admiring her handiwork, Candace thought Lindsay could pass as a poster child for a cowgirl.

When the bell rang, Lindsay screamed and raced to the door. She hopped from one leg to the other, anxious for Candace to hurry up and open it.

Solae glided inside and *ooh*ed and *ahh*ed over Lindsay's outfit before squatting and giving her goddaughter a hug and kiss. Standing, Solae greeted Candace in the same manner.

As was the norm, Solae made casual dress into a fashion statement. She wore the warmest shade of blue that made her skin glow. She eyed Candace's attire at the same time, a denim jumper and flats—plain and simple.

Twisting her mouth, Solae practically circled her. "I

guess you'll pass," she teased. "We definitely need to work on updating your wardrobe."

"Thanks," Candace said dryly. "I love you, too." She couldn't help it that her casual clothes were really casual. She didn't go out and now that she was working outside the home, she was building her business wardrobe.

"Come on, Mommy and Aunt Sollie, I don't want to miss my turn on the horsy!"

Playfully snatching the car keys out of Candace's hand, Solae juggled hers. "I'm driving. There's a strip mall near the birthday party with a café and boutique shops for us to window shop." She grinned.

Since Solae kept an extra booster seat in her car, Candace didn't have an objection to riding with her. After she swiped their sweaters off the sofa along with the child's gift, Candace locked the front door. In the car, Solae programmed the party address in her GPS and pulled away from the driveway.

Lindsay entertained them with details about who was having a birthday party next. "Ryan says he will have clowns and Jasmine is going to have a tea party."

"You're going to be broke," Solae murmured, exchanging glances with Candace.

"Tell me about it."

After thirty minutes of singing songs and Solae quizzing Lindsay on her numbers and alphabet, they turned off the highway to a gravel road. They couldn't miss Terrence's Ranch as they followed the big signs and balloons along the path.

"Remember, in and out," Solae reminded Candace again, making herself a temporary parking space at the ranch's entrance. "Introduce yourself, make sure the children will be supervised properly on the horses, and leave…"

Tuning her friend out, Candace unstrapped Lindsay from her booster seat and helped her out the car as Solae continued to give orders. "Five minutes—seven tops—anything beyond a second longer," Solae lowered her voice, so Lindsay wouldn't hear, "I have no shame in crashing a child's party."

Lindsay soon forgot about both of them as her eyes widened with excitement at the kiddie carnival rides. It was almost as if parents were trying to outdo each other with the grandeur of their parties. From the balloons to the animals, there was no doubt that Brandon's family had gone all the way out for his birthday celebration.

"Bye, Aunt Sollie." Lindsay waved and skipped ahead of Candace, who held the child's present in her arms.

Solae honked and Candace twirled around. "I mean it, Candy," using a childhood nickname that only surfaced when she was serious.

"I know." Annoyed with her friend's pestering, Candace gritted her teeth and hurried to catch up with her daughter to get it over with.

They were almost at the front porch when Lindsay made a beeline to a little boy who waved at them furiously. Suddenly, the front door swung open. The firefighter from career day filled the entryway, appearing larger than life. Immediately, she noted he had shaved, which made him look different from when she first saw him. Why did the absence of his five o'clock shadow disappoint her?

Wow. Candace swallowed. She thought he was handsome in the helmet and jacket, but wearing jeans and a wrinkle-free shirt, he was temptation she hadn't confronted in years. His bulging muscles were evidence of the strength he possessed to carry someone away from a burning building.

"Hello," Candace found her voice. Whether it was just hot or her deodorant wasn't working, something was the source of her perspiration.

"Hello, Miss Clark, I was hoping you would come, actually praying that you would." He seemed relieved as he stepped forward. Not only was he built, but he stood majestically over her five-foot-five frame. This was one of those times Candace wished she had worn her three inch heels.

"You remembered my name?" she asked, somewhat flattered.

"Your name, your face and that cute little daughter of yours." His boyish smile added to his overpowering masculinity. "I'm Royce Kavanaugh." Extending his hand, Royce swallowed up hers in a secure, but gentle embrace as his eyes kept hers captive.

"Ah…Candace Clark."

"Beautiful…named after the Ethiopian queen in the book of Acts," he said, almost in awe.

She had never been compared to a queen and the African connection was even more flattering, considering he linked it to the Bible. She would have blushed, but his adoration turned into a stern expression, definitely meant to intimidate.

"You had me worried about you."

"Pardon me?" She frowned.

"I'm the firefighter who caught you when you collapsed from the stress of witnessing the little boy who got hit on his bicycle. After we made sure he was okay, I didn't mind being the one to rescue you." He winked.

She didn't want to replay the events of that day at all. Of course, she didn't remember seeing him. Royce's handsome looks would stay a lifetime in a woman's memory bank, but somehow he wasn't in hers; she had probably been in shock. She looked away, not wanting to relive that day, and her morning prayers with Solae were helping her to conquer those fears. "Thank you." She left it at that.

"You're more than welcome." His voice was husky as he trapped in her a stare.

When she managed to blink, Royce cleared his throat and excused himself, leaving her standing there. He disappeared into the house and returned with a bouquet of flowers and determination in his eyes until he gave them to her; then his stern expression softened.

"For you."

Whispering her thanks, Candace closed her eyes to sniff the fragrance and caught a whiff of his cologne. Exactly who was the guest of honor at this party—her or Brandon Kavanaugh?

She doubted Solae would have set this up. Her friend knew better than to mastermind a blind date. Neither of them cared for surprises like that.

Taking a deep breath, Candace faced him again. "What if I hadn't come?"

"My sister-in-law would have enjoyed them, but you did. I was so enthralled the first time I saw you as a crossing guard while on our way to a fire…"

A fire truck? She wondered if that was her first day on the assignment. "You aren't the one who whistled at me, are you?" She lifted a brow.

And he had the nerve to look chastened. "You mean I

was the only one who temporarily lost my mind?"

Royce raised his hand. "Guilty. You were a distraction then just as you are now. I was relieved when you walked in the door on Career Day. Not only did you survive the ordeal with Tommy, but I couldn't take my eyes off you. You didn't need that safety vest to stop traffic."

Career Day. How many embarrassments would she suffer in front of this man? "Well, thank you, I'm sure that run in my stocking was also a focal point. If I remember correctly, you smirked when you looked at my legs." She arched a manicured brow.

Lifting a silky brow, Royce's nostrils flared. "Trust me, you complemented that run. It did nothing to take away from your appearance. You were captivating to me and the class," he assured her. "And I noticed the day you fell in my arms, at school and today, you aren't wearing a ring, I take that as you're not married, so I hope my compliments are not out of line."

They were thick. *He's flirting with me and I'm at a loss for words.* It wasn't as if men hadn't flirted with her since Daniel's death, but with Lindsay by her side or in her arms to act as a buffer, many didn't pursue it.

But turnabout was fair play. Through the hood of her lashes, she glanced at his ring finger—nothing, but that meant nothing, too. Not every husband felt obligated to wear a ring. Her husband wore his with pride. She needed to change the subject. "Is Brandon your son?"

"No, my nephew. I'm not married nor do I have any children." He offered the tidbit without her daring to ask. "My brother is the fire captain and got tied up at the station on Career Day. I stood in as his replacement. Imagine how I felt seeing the woman I rescued at center stage."

Suddenly, Candace remembered they were not alone, why she was there and Solae's threat. She knew her friend would have no problem carrying it out. "Well, thank you again for the flowers, but I have to go. Do you mind if I take a look at the ponies and who is steering them? I know...I'm a control freak; I need to be in control of my daughter's environment, especially when I'm not around. Just call me a parent freak."

"No, you just love your daughter." Invading her private space, Royce moved closer and removed the gift from her arm that she had forgotten she was holding. Candace was surprised Royce hadn't caused her to forget her name.

"You don't have to rush off. Stay."

Although Royce's words were soft, his good looks couldn't mask the tiredness in his eyes. She suddenly felt the urge to pamper him. Blame it on her nurturing instincts, but she refrained herself from acting impulsively with a stranger.

There was this unexplainable connection that made her want to stay and not just to watch over Lindsay. "I can't. My friend is waiting for me in the car. I'm sorry."

Making no attempts to rein in his disappointment, Royce rubbed his jaw—the clean shaven one. "I see. Well, your friend—he—is invited to stay, too. There is plenty of food and room."

Laughing to cover her nervousness, Candace may have been out of the game since Daniel, but she knew the game Royce was playing. "Believe me, one look at Solae and you'll bite your tongue. She could never be mistaken for a he."

"I don't need to look. I don't believe in window

shopping if my attention is elsewhere."

Whew. Now her palms were sweaty. The man was unstoppable. Instead of putting out a fire, he was kindling her emotions. She had to exhale to keep from fainting. "How flattering, but my friend and I have planned an afternoon to eat and shop—"

"Candace, we have plenty of food, excellent company…" He gave her a lopsided smile. "If your daughter's father is not in your life or you're not seeing anybody, I would love for us to get to know each other over dinner, the movies, skating."

She opened her mouth, but nothing came out right away.

"Please stay."

"Either he was moving too fast or she too slow, but she couldn't process the unexpected conversation. "My friend and Lindsay's godmother will come looking for me. She has no problem making a scene and repenting later."

"I ain't scared." Royce shivered and coaxed a smile out of her. "Come on, let's see if I can convince her to let you stay and play."

"Right." She chuckled at how ironic it was that Solae was the one always pushing her to get out and meet someone, and the one man who she found to be confident, charming and fascinating—did she say fine—happened to be at a child's birthday party.

Candace was curious how this man could be so sure of his infatuation when they really hadn't spent much time together. Craning her neck, she spied her daughter who was in a line, waiting for a clown to paint color art on her face.

"Well…ok—"

"Great!" Adjusting the gift to the other arm, Royce

touched her elbow and unhurriedly escorted her down the pathway, retracing her steps. Candace expected Solae to be outside her car, marching in her heels to meet her halfway. Candace squinted. Evidently, she was the last thing on Solae's agenda.

"Is that your friend next to that silver car? If so, then it appears my older brother has detained her. "That's Brandon's father, Captain Hershel Kavanaugh," Royce said with pride in his voice.

No wonder she hasn't come looking for me. Candace smiled, recognizing the admiration the man had for his brother. As an only child, she had wished for more children for Lindsay, but that hope was dashed.

As they approached, neither Hershel nor Solae looked their way. As a matter of fact, Solae seemed startled when Candace called her name. Jumping, Solae stood at attention as if she had been caught buying Victoria's Secret underwear and the pastor snuck up on her.

"Huh? Oh. Hey, Candace."

Royce's brother never looked their way, instead he continued to watch Solae.

What was it with these Kavanaugh men, holding women captive and with such intensity until a woman lost her mind? Their testosterone levels definitely needed to be checked and serviced.

"This is Brandon's father and he's invited us to stay," Solae said as if Candace hadn't figured out the reason she had not yet dragged her away from there. Her coy smile meant they would talk later. Definitely, because her friend very seldom changed her mind when it came to shopping.

Now who was going to babysit whom? And she didn't mean Lindsay. Solae didn't date outside their faith and neither of them knew anything about these brothers, including their commitments to God. "Really?"

"I guess it's settled, ladies. It looks like the party is just getting started," Hershel said as he led Solae away from her car.

For some reason, Candace had a suspicion that the party he referred to had nothing to do with a five-year-old's birthday party.

Chapter 12

"I guess you never can have too many chaperones," Candace said, accepting the invitation.

Chaperones were not what Royce had in mind, not after pining for Candace for weeks. He was definitely thinking in terms of something more private as Royce did a quick sweep of her attire.

Whereas Solae was pretty, Candace was a knockout. Her legs elevated her to another level—gorgeous—because every woman didn't have legs that would catch a man's eye.

The outfit she wore showcased them perfectly—a denim form-fitting dress with matching jacket and flats that reminded him of a ballerina.

They strolled past the front door of the ranch house that belonged to his cousin, Terrence, to the back lawn where the activity was nonstop. More than thirty children, including most of the children in Brandon's class, formed lines to be next for their turn to ride on the pony.

Staying close by her side, Royce watched as Candace acknowledged the other parents she knew. "It's good to see so many fathers with their children. At least I'm not the only single parent in the bunch."

"Oh no, you're not. Whether you know it or not, my brother is divorced and is rearing my nephews alone."

It was noteworthy that Hershel had become so instantly smitten with Candace's friend. It took more than an attractive face to get his attention as Hershel always reminded him and Trent. *Me and my kids are the ones who got burned by a trifling woman. And I'm praying every night to keep me from becoming bitter. I mean, what type of woman leaves her children? Pretty women are nothing but trouble.* would spill out from the depths of Hershel's soul from time to time.

After ditching Candace's gift on the table where others were displayed, he guided her to a pair of lawn loungers off to the side for some privacy.

Once Candace made her choice, Royce took the other. His body sunk into the uncomfortable lounger as he stretched out his long legs. A yawn escaped as he thought about the sleep he was sacrificing to be there with her.

"Sorry." He covered his mouth.

"Did you fight fires last night?"

"Yes, and there were other calls, too." Royce did his best not to yawn again. Maybe sitting still wasn't a good idea.

"Then why are you here instead of sleeping? You look tired."

Her concern, frown, and slight scolding were endearing. "Whether I'm a firefighter or not, I'm expected to be at my nephew's party. Orders from my sister-in-law and brother."

"With so many children, I doubt if you would be missed for the couple of hours it would take for you to get some rest." She scrutinized him.

Yes, Royce could see himself as the beneficiary of her

pampering. "I had to come to see you again. Sometimes a person only gets one last chance, especially in my line of work."

She took on an unreadable expression. "You don't have to have a dangerous job to live each day as if it's your last chance to say or do things," she whispered, amazing him with her understanding.

"I guess this is a little late, but to clear my conscience I have to ask…is Lindsay's father out of the picture, or is there a chance for reconciliation where I need to step aside?"

He willed her to say that there were no obstacles. Royce watched her body language for his answer before she even uttered a sound.

Although he was very attracted to her physically, family was important and he believed every man should do the right thing. If only Hershel had let him use Brandon to scout around for information.

As he waited, Candace's eyes teared up. Immediately, Royce's slumped body went on alert. Maybe Lindsay's father had put her through some kind of drama and it was painful for her to talk about it.

Gritting his teeth, Royce felt guilty for stirring up those emotions. It took all his willpower not to reach out and comfort her.

Sniffing, Candace mustered a weak smile. "Lindsay never met her father. Daniel was a good man, husband and would have made a great father, but he was killed crossing the street three months before she was born," Candace quietly explained, bowing her head.

"Jesus gave me comfort. Prayer and counseling gave me strength. Without question, Solae and her mother have been my support system."

"I'm sorry to hear that about your late husband. I can't imagine how you must feel. That child's accident must have caused the memories of your own personal loss to resurface."

There was so much he wanted to know about her. Royce documented her every movement and expression. From the rapid batting of her lashes, Royce guessed she was fighting back the pain. This was not what he envisioned for their first real meeting.

As the silence stretched between them, Royce battled his brain on how to recover the light conversation they shared before her revelation.

Candace smiled again. This time it was genuine. "You made a lasting impression on Lindsay. I've learned more fire prevention tips listening to her than I have watching crime shows."

"Good for her." Royce winked. "So what's your favorite show?"

"Law & Order."

"Good choice."

"But you were the hero on Career Day. Lindsay said all the girls liked the lady dancer, but everybody liked Mr. Firefighter because you brought them stickers, coloring books and other goodies."

As if she heard her name, Lindsay skipped up to them. The neat little girl who arrived to the party had vanished, replaced by this one with dirt on previously pristine white top and strands of thick black hair that had escaped a hairband.

After hugging her mother, she hesitated, looking at Royce. "Hi, Mr. Fireman." She waved, but didn't leave Candace's side.

"Hi Lindsay, don't you look cute today," Royce said, making the girl bashful.

"What do you say?" Her mother prompted while gently tugging on her daughter's ponytail.

Giggling, Lindsay thanked him, then took off as if she was merely checking in or checking up on her mother. Candace watched as she rejoined a group of girls.

Royce observed the tenderness between them, wondering if there would be room for him to squeeze in as a third wheel. He had an edict never to get involved with another woman who had a child. It was easier to end a relationship if children weren't a factor. But that was before Candace. If it wasn't for her sweet little girl, Royce would have never met her.

He got caught staring when she faced him again. A ray of sunshine captured and highlighted her pretty brown eyes. "Have you ever been married or do you have any children?" She switched the tables on him.

Linking his hands together, Royce shook his head. "No, I've never been a husband or father, but I'm told I'm a great uncle."

He grinned; she chuckled, then she began to toy with him. "Let me guess. You haven't found the right one or you're not ready or…"

"The right one…hmm." He stroked the rough hairs on his chin. "That's an easy one. God could put me in a room full of dozens of beautiful Christian women, but the one I would seek would not only be pleasing to the eye, but also a sweet praying woman."

"Christ is my backbone. He has provided for me and scolded me. I try to practice what my pastor preaches about how without holiness no one can see God. I didn't understand that until I received the baptism in water in Jesus' name and His Holy Ghost. That's who I am," she sounded defensive. "Besides, there are plenty of women in every church. I'm sure yours is no exception."

"True." *But I'm not sitting here talking to them.* "Every Christian doesn't know how to fast and pray. She also has to be comfortable with my absences because of my long shifts and rejoice when I come home. Not every woman wants that type of sacrifice."

A youngster's squeal pulled Candace's attention away from him. She fumbled with her fingers before meeting his stare. "Why me?"

"You got my attention. Forgive me if I'm coming off as overbearing, but I've wanted to get to know you for almost a month. Today was my chance and I took it."

Candace sucked in her breath, following his honest admission. She seemed to give what he was saying some thought.

"I'm flattered, but I don't know if I am the one. I went from being a bride to becoming a wife to being a widow and then a mother. I've lived a lifetime before I reached twenty-four years old."

"Yes, you have," Royce said softly, realizing the magnitude of the trials she had faced. "And I'm sure you've come to this point in your life because you know how to pray."

"Have you ever dated a woman with a child?" Did she ask to challenge his insecurities or was she oblivious to them?

He squirmed in his seat. "I have, and to be honest with you, I didn't feel good when the relationships were over. I was as much a part of the children's lives as their mothers, and they were heartbroken."

"Thank you for sharing that. I appreciate your honesty." She had a tender, but unreadable expression that didn't hint where he stood after his last statement. "My daughter's happiness means everything to me. I was an only child and so was Daniel. Lindsay doesn't have any grandparents unless I count Miss Minerva—Solae's mom. My child needs stability and I don't see how dating one guy after another one will give her that."

If that was her attempt at pushing him away, it was useless. No water or chemical could smother the fire she had ignited in him. Royce was not only a praying man, but a determined one, too.

I just feel that you're the one, he thought, *but I can't just blurt that out. The woman may already think I'm a stalker.* "I'm not asking you to date a string of other men, just me."

Royce took advantage when she stalled in her response. "Candace, you are too young and too beautiful not to have your own happiness. You can't live your life vicariously through your daughter's. I would like to take you to dinner and a movie."

Feeling mischievous, he pressed her. "But if you won't go out with Mr. Fireman, maybe that pretty little cowgirl over there," he pointed in the direction where Lindsay and the others were playing, "will accept my date for a McDonald's Happy Meal and a matinee—have to be mindful of her bedtime—and I'll even let you tag along."

Candace's roar of laughter was contagious. Royce chuckled until he joined in along with her.

"I think my daughter is too young to date, Fireman Kavanaugh." She wrinkled her nose in a tease that was seductive.

Royce could be just as seductive as he lowered his voice. "I have no problem with you being our chaperone." He winked.

She was beautiful when she blushed. "I need to give this some thought. I can't just jump into the dating pool without any reservations. Your flattery is catching me off guard."

He stifled another yawn. He was losing steam. "Miss Clark, you're the finest crossing guard I've ever seen. I already told you I had to take advantage of each day and make my intentions known."

"Even if it means sacrificing the sleep that it looks like you're craving now?"

"What other way could I impress a lady?" His grin was weak. Royce was beat, but he pressed on. "Here's my number... I'm a firefighter and I'll use a ladder to climb into your heart if necessary."

Resting his case, Royce could no longer resist closing his eyes for a brief moment.

Chapter 13

No, he didn't. Any other man who dozed off in the middle of a discussion, Candace wouldn't dare forget. Actually, she felt sorry for him. Clearly Royce was tired.

If Candace was a teacher, she would give him an A+ for effort, not only for being there for his nephew, but also for admitting he wanted to see her.

Something within her wouldn't let her desert him. As he drifted deeper into a peaceful slumber, she admired his raw handsomeness. Candace was content just to stay by his side and let his soft snores lull her.

How he could sleep in the midst of childish screams, giggles and pleadings for more pony rides was amazing.

When Lindsay came barreling her way, Candace put a finger to her lips, so as not to wake Royce. Her daughter complied, bobbing her head.

Although Lindsay appeared almost out of breath, the jubilance spread across her face and the odor that came with being around animals was evidence that she was having a good time.

For no other reason than love, Lindsay wrapped her

arms around Candace's neck. After two tight squeezes, she took off again. She smiled at her daughter's antics. Candace had been truthful about Lindsay's happiness meaning everything to her.

Leaning back in her chair, she studied Royce's features again: a neatly trimmed mustache against smooth pecan brown skin, wide set eyes with curly lashes, full lips, a strong, masculine chin, and an unquestionably conditioned build.

He also had the even breathing of a man who was fast asleep. What woman wouldn't be giddy, receiving his attention?

To date or not to date wasn't such a simple question. If it didn't work, who would suffer the greatest heartache— she or Lindsay? But the deeper question was what if—God forbid—Royce got hurt, or worse, killed in the line of duty? Then what?

Men ought to always pray and not faint, the wind carried the words in Luke 18:1.

She immediately looked at Royce who was fast asleep, then realized the source—Jesus.

As the words revolved in her mind, she thought back to the day of Tommy's accident when she fainted. Was that a sign that she wasn't prayed up? *God help me*.

It seemed what mattered most to Royce beyond the looks was a woman who knew how to reach the throne of God with prayers. Had she overcome her fears enough to believe God when she prayed that He would do whatever she asked in Jesus' name? Royce left her with so many questions that were aside from dating.

It wasn't fair for Royce to be resting while stirring up unrest in her spirit. She looked away from his sleeping form as she spied out Solae, who along with Royce's brother, were laughing at one of the children's antics.

She watched their interaction. They seemed to be so comfortable in each other's presence as if they had known each other for years instead of hours, but Solae had that down to earth personality.

Royce and Hershel were both tall, handsome men, but they didn't look much alike. She wondered what happened in Hershel's marriage that it ended in divorce.

Solae would definitely find out. Absentmindedly swinging her arm over the armrest, she brushed Royce's hand.

With quickness, he encircled her hand, trapping it in a firm, but gentle hold. Nothing else moved: his eyes, head, or a snore. It was an almost sub-conscious reaction, as if he knew she was still there.

Royce's unexpected touch felt natural, so much so that she didn't bother to break free. Their hands remained connected throughout the opening of the gifts, cutting of the cake, and even Lindsay needing to go to the potty.

Candace whispered her assurance to her daughter that she was a big girl and could go on her own. Soon the party was over and surprisingly, Candace was more disappointed than Lindsay when it was time to leave.

Glancing at Royce while disengaging their hands, Candace thought about his heartfelt request. Although she wasn't looking nor felt ready to date, Royce's spiritual request fascinated her. Getting to her feet, she whispered into his ear, "The party's over. I enjoyed talking to you."

Surprisingly, Royce stirred and struggled to open one eye, but was unsuccessful.

"Good night, baby," he murmured and rolled on his side.

Shocked, Candace's heart fluttered at the unexpected uttered endearment. That subconscious slip of the lips reminded her of what it felt like to belong to someone, to be loved. It had, indeed, been so long.

When Solae and Hershel headed her way, Candace intercepted him from waking Royce.

His brother seemed to mull over her request. "Okay, but he's not going to be happy that he didn't see you off."

"He gave me his number. I can call him."

Hershel grunted. "Make sure you do; my brother can be very stubborn." He didn't hint of a forthcoming smile. "I'll walk you lovely ladies to your car."

Lindsay picked that moment to whine. "Mommy, I can't walk." Her flushed face and droopy eyes were the telltale signs that having fun was exhausting.

She was still lightweight, so Candace bent to scoop her up, but Hershel offered his assistance. With ease, he lifted Lindsay in his arms, carried her to Solae's car and strapped her into her booster seat.

"Thanks for keeping me company today," Hershel said softly to Solae as Candace eavesdropped.

"It was fun. I'm glad I stayed. Children are a blessing, even with their runny noses, temper tantrums and nonstop energy…they're a blessing," Solae responded as Hershel waited for her to get behind the wheel, then shut her door. Hershel waved and stepped back as Solae started the ignition and he watched them drive away.

Moments later, Solae said in a hushed tone, "I was definitely wrong."

Double-checking that Lindsay was asleep, Candace asked, "What do you mean?"

"Royce Kavanaugh was definitely smitten and from the

look of things, you weren't consumed about Lindsay's every movement for a change."

Candace tried not to blush. "Royce? I thought you were referring to Hershel, and how would you know that Miss I'm Coming to Look for You in Five Minutes, only to be lured away by Captain Kavanaugh."

Angling her body toward Solae, Candace folded her arms and waited for her friend to come clean about the immediate attraction between her and Hershel.

Gripping the steering wheel, Solae sighed with a blissful expression. She chanced a look at Candace before turning off the gravel road onto a main street. "That is one fine man. Humph!"

"I've never known you to date an ugly one, so…" Candace paused, hoping Solae would pick it up from there. She didn't, so Candace prompted her. "What was it about him that made you give him the time of day?"

Shrugging, she exhaled. "Honestly, I don't know. It's like I could connect with bits and pieces of him, if that makes any sense."

"Like?"

"Without saying a word, we recognized the attraction was there and we didn't play games. It happened so unexpectedly. You and Lindsay hadn't been gone a minute when he came up to my car with an attitude saying, 'You can't park here.' I turned around with my game face to let him know I wasn't parking, but waiting to leave."

Solae changed lanes, then continued, "When our eyes met, it seemed as if we both backed down. After a few minutes I felt I didn't need to act coy and he didn't seem interested in running a game on me. It was as if we enjoyed the moment, not knowing what was coming next."

"Wow." Kavanaugh brothers seemed to live in the moment as if every second counted.

"Okay, what about you and Royce? Don't think I didn't see you two holding hands and you barely left his side—no, correction—you didn't leave his side. Hmm-mm."

"How did you see all that when it appeared you were occupied yourself?"

"I know how to multi-task, minding my business and yours, too." She snickered. "So are you going to see Royce again?"

"If I let him have his way, probably. He gave me his number." She frowned. "Surprisingly, Royce wants beauty and a blessed woman who can pray through a crisis...I don't know if I'm at that point in my life where I've conquered all my insecurities to be that one. And that's only one of my concerns. The bad thing is I can really see myself falling for him and that scares me."

"Maybe, you're looking at the physical challenge of the relationship only, but Royce comes along with a spiritual challenge. Prayer changes things. Don't run away from this one. He may be here to stay."

They were both quiet, lost in their thoughts. Candace was reminded of the heartaches Solae had suffered in a few relationships where the man professed his love, but walked once she confided the devastating news.

Those jerks never looked back. Candace swallowed the hurt she felt for her friend.

Clearing her throat, Solae straightened her shoulders. "And second?"

"I was hoping you had forgotten that one," Candace mumbled, closed her eyes and rushed through her other concern.

"One loss in a lifetime is one too many; God knows I can't bear two. What if he gets…" she couldn't say it.

"God knows everything that happens in our life is for a reason. I know you lost Daniel suddenly and the same thing can happen again with any man, not just firefighters.

"The fact is there are many firefighters who retire after a long successful career. My inability to bear children is my fate in this world, but to paraphrase Job 15:13, 'Yet will I trust Him'. I have to believe His grace is enough for me, so what's your excuse?"

Candace twisted her lips in defeat. "I guess I don't have one."

Chapter 14

A few days had passed and Candace had yet to make that call, but Royce was never far from her mind. Not only did he seem genuine and a man committed to God, but Royce was intense and distractingly handsome. She smiled as she prepared lunches for her and Lindsay. Prior to the previous week, Candace hadn't a concern about having a man in her life.

Whenever a fire truck whizzed by her since meeting Royce, she thought about what above all Royce desired; a praying woman was at the top of the list.

Unbeknownst to him, he had been the force behind her and Solae increasing their prayer time in the mornings. So why hadn't she called, even though Candace had memorized his number? *I just can't rush this.*

"Who are you talking to, Mommy?" Lindsay asked, walking up behind her.

Candace jumped, and seeing her daughter, forced herself back to the present. "Oh, thinking out loud I guess, baby..." She eyed her child's feet.

"Take off your shoes and put on your socks. Hurry up now, so we won't be late." Lindsay seemed to be dragging.

Her enthusiasm to go to school had waned in favor of more sleep.

By the time Lindsay was dressed to meet Candace's standards; they were already behind schedule, and rushing out the door.

The traffic and the synchronized lights seemed to be on her side as she headed the short distance to Duncan Elementary School. With five minutes to spare, Candace parked in her regular slot, helped Lindsay out the back seat and grabbed her crossing guard gear.

Thanks to the numerous weekend parties, Lindsay had made many friends and Candace felt comfortable allowing Lindsay to walk across the small campus with her classmates.

After successfully leading two troops of children across the intersection, the sun seemed to blink and go into hiding. Loud voices preceded another group of children walking in an unhurried pace toward her.

Candace had just stepped off the curb with her stop sign when she felt a drop. In her mad dash to get to school, she had left her umbrella at home. "Great."

Once she was out of the intersection, Candace looked up in the sky as clouds rumbled. Yep, she was definitely going to get drenched.

There went the hairstyle makeover Solae had given her the other day with the soft bouncy curls. Her coworkers had raved about her new look.

As the second and third drops trickled down her face, Candace braced herself for the downpour. By the time she got to the office, Candace would either look a mess or fashionable like Chaka Khan.

She still had students coming from two directions and

she couldn't abandon her post because of the weather. At least some had umbrellas or were wearing ponchos.

Note to self, she thought, *when removing the umbrella from the car, remember to return it or buy an extra.*

Glancing over shoulder to make sure there were no stragglers, Candace blinked, then squinted. *Royce?* He was still wearing his uniform and heading her way.

His swagger was even more welcome than the umbrella he was holding, which was big enough to hold a family of four.

Her heart pounded with excitement. It wasn't a fire, but it appeared he had come to rescue her. Sucking in her breath, Candace could only watch as he kept walking until he invaded her space, towering over her with the umbrella.

"Sorry, I'm late," he said.

She frowned. "For what?

"Not getting here before the storm." It was as if his words cued the windows of heaven to release the downpour, but he protected her.

Leaning into him, under the guise of staying dry, Candace giggled as he pulled her closer. When the last school bell rang, she did another head check for any little ones. None in sight.

Escorting her back to the lot where she was parked, Royce practically lifted her off her feet to help her avoid a puddle.

She reveled in his strength as she looked into his eyes, but what she saw there gave her pause.

His handsomeness couldn't hide his exhaustion. It seemed that instead of going home for what she suspected was much-needed rest, he'd thought about her. It was the second time he had foregone sleep to see her. She felt cherished.

"Thank you," she whispered.

His lopsided smile was another one of her rewards. "Sorry I didn't call."

Embarrassed, she looked away when she admitted, "I never gave you my number."

He grunted. "Did you think that small technicality would stop me from seeing you again?"

She bowed her head, so he wouldn't see her blush. She was glad it didn't.

"Candace, don't make me come here every morning whether in a fire truck or on foot to see you, because I will."

The intensity of his stare made a believer out of her. "My days have been shortened. Another parent has been assigned to alternating days with me, so instead of every day, I'll only have Tuesdays and Thursdays."

"Duly noted. Now, back to us...I'd rather take you to someplace nice and dry where I'm holding your hand instead of an umbrella. I've already told you I have no problem taking Lindsay along on our dates if that will make you more comfortable."

She was too embarrassed to admit that it would.

His nostrils seemed to expand with excitement. "Since silence is golden, I'll take that as a yes."

Closing her eyes, Candace took a deep breath. She was going to go for it.

"If you keep your eyes closed a second longer, I'm kissing you."

Candace's lids fluttered open. Royce's smirk clearly read, "Yeah, I said it."

"You're serious, aren't you?" Suddenly, she realized that she liked being chased. It was empowering.

"About the dates with Lindsay—yes, about kissing

you—most definitely, but only with your permission. I was reared a gentlemen, and since I surrendered to God's way, there's no way I would displease Him or you."

She was happy to see that there were still gentlemen in that day and time. "Can I pinch you? I want to make sure you're real." She squinted as Royce laughed and flexed his muscles for her to do the honors.

Although she was enjoying this moment with him, she had to get to work. Playfully pinching him, they both chuckled. "How about having our first date at Chuck E. Cheese's?"

Royce lifted a brow. "I like pizza."

"Then it's a date." He opened her door and she reached for a piece of paper and scribbled her number and address. "I won't tell Lindsay about *her* first date in case you need to reschedule because of work."

"Only a fire or Jesus coming back for His saints would stop me from being there."

Starting the ignition in her car and social life, Candace gave him a smile. "Duly noted."

Chapter 15

Candace's sweet fragrance lingered as Royce watched her drive away. Wanting every memory of her to last, he inhaled deeply.

One thing was for sure, their attraction was mutual and he was wearing her defenses down.

He briefly reflected on the eight verses in Revelation that mention the promises that follow overcoming.

Indeed, Royce looked forward to whatever blessing He had in store for him and Candace.

"And to think I almost missed my blessing because of a hang-up about not dating another single mother."

He shook his head in disbelief at his stupidity as he climbed into his own vehicle and stretched his muscles.

Twenty minutes later, Royce called Hershel seconds after walking through the door. Despite his excitement over the latest developments with Candace, Royce didn't talk or text while driving.

He and his crew had rescued too many people who had— some with fatal consequences.

"She said yes," Royce dived right in as soon as his brother answered, "albeit at Chuck E. Cheese's, but that's better than White Castle's. The consequences of those onions on the burgers probably wouldn't guarantee me a second date."

Hershel roared. "Solae suggested Dave & Buster's for our first date and the boys loved it."

Kicking off his shoes en route to his bedroom, Royce next angled the phone between his shoulder and ear to remove his shirt. "I never thought you would give another woman a chance."

"She had so much patience with the children at the party, including mine. It got to a point where the children were coming to her, whether for punch or a problem. Solae is something else, and since it was the spur of the moment, I don't think she was trying to impress me…"

Royce listened without interrupting. It was interesting to hear his brother so taken with another woman. There was no mistaking Hershel's happiness.

"With her sweet personality, I'm surprised no one has snatched her up. She's never been married and doesn't have children. She definitely is mother material, judging from how the children took to her."

He paused. "So I guess we're thinking along the same lines, because I never thought you would give another single mother the time of day."

Eying the pile of dirty clothes in his hamper, Royce made a note to wash after he got eight plus hours of sleep.

"It would have been my loss," Royce admitted as he padded to the kitchen for a bagel and a glass of juice. "She was very understanding; she left some leeway for our date in case I needed to cancel because of work."

"Then she's probably a keeper," had been his brother's

last word a few minutes later as exhaustion hit, and Royce signed off.

After his shower, Royce read a verse, then knelt for his prayers. "Lord, I thank You for everything in my life, but especially for covering me with Your blood while responding to situations only You can control. And most of all, thank You for filling my loneliness with Candace and Lindsay. I trust You to guide our relationship. In Jesus' name. Amen."

Royce burrowed under the covers as if preparing for hibernation. The last vision in his mind was of him and Candace under the umbrella. "Come on Chuck E. Cheese's."

"Do you realize that this is the first time in a long time, we've both been in a relationship at the same time and we've never dated brothers or cousins?" Solae asked minutes after Candace replayed her conversation with Royce.

"Hold up. I haven't really crossed over the dating threshold. I'm just testing the waters," Candace said, then turned around to type in her password to retrieve her accounts.

A peppermint bounced off her shoulder. "Ouch, girl. Stop it. I'm trying to work." Candace twirled around in her chair.

"No, you stop it," Solae said, walking into Candace's cubicle. Leaning on the partition, she crossed her arms. "Let Mr. Fireman woo you. I'm definitely enjoying Hershel's attention, and his boys are so adorable."

Candace lowered her voice. "Has he told you what happened between him and his ex-wife?"

Looking both ways over her shoulder, Solae shook her head. "Only that his ex had an extramarital affair and she left him."

Covering her mouth, Candace gasped. "What? She walked away from that hunk and cute boys? Wow. I think there needs to be an addendum to the scriptures. In addition to 'He that findeth a wife, findeth a good thing', I think 'She that getteth a husband, getteth a good thing' should be penciled in."

"I know, right?" Solae frowned. "Finding a man who loves you is a premium, finding a good father is priceless...what I wouldn't give for that..." she sighed with a wishful downcast look, then recovered. "

Anyway, be happy. Both brothers are practicing Christians. That's a major plus in this day and age." She returned to her desk without another word.

The rest of Candace's day was uneventful until she was about to leave work for her afternoon crossing guard duties when she received a text.

Be careful crossing the street, pretty lady. I can't wait to see you again. Royce

She smiled and stared at the message before texting him back: I will. I hope you had sweet dreams.

I did, and you were in them. I'm off the next two days. I can't wait to see my old friend, Chuck E.

Candace bit her lip to keep a laugh from escaping.

How about tomorrow around five-thirty?

It's a date! It had been five years in the making, and truth be told, Candace couldn't wait and she hummed all the way to the car. *Lord, did I tell You thank you today? Thank You!*

Hours later, Royce was still on her mind as she

prepared dinner while Lindsay did her homework at the kitchen table.

Tomorrow was exactly twenty-four hours away. Candace couldn't stand it any longer. She grabbed her smartphone and sent Royce a text.

I hope I'm not disturbing you, but I never thanked you for thinking about me this morning and making sure I arrived at work dry and intact. C.

Seconds after hitting send, Candace was stirring the pasta when her cell phone rang. She smiled, guessing it was Royce.

"Who's that Mommy?" Lindsay asked before she could say hello.

"You can never disturb me. I've been thinking about you nonstop since this morning. There's something about you that makes me want to protect you from the storms as the Lord gives me the strength."

Blushing, Candace turned her back to Lindsay. He always made her heart flutter. She covered the phone and faced her daughter. "Put that up for now, sweetie and go wash your hands so you can eat."

"But I already washed my hands, Mommy." She lifted them for her to see.

Smart kid. "Ok, then put your homework up for now."

Closing her folder, Lindsay folded her hands like an obedient student, but she didn't budge from her chair. Her daughter wasn't going anywhere and Candace wasn't one to leave her alone in the kitchen with hot pots on the stove. *So much for privacy.*

"Take care of her," Royce said patiently. "I'll be available whenever you call."

"Thank you for understanding." She lowered her

voice. Gnawing on her lip, she marveled that this was the first time in a long time she really craved the soothing voice of another man.

"Soon," she murmured into the phone, then she reluctantly said good-bye before enjoying dinner with Lindsay, but she was definitely looking forward to pizza the next night.

Chapter 16

The next morning, Candace woke, counting the hours before she saw Royce again. Solae said she was glowing when she strutted into the office and was downright giddy when she left for her crossing guard duties.

Lindsay learned that they were going out to eat when Candace explained why she was getting a snack instead of dinner. Her daughter had no clue that they both were about to go on a date.

Now with one hour and twenty-nine minutes before she saw Royce, Solae called to add her two cents.

"What are you wearing? Never mind." She *tsk*ed. "Put on your purple dress and make sure you use your eyebrow pencil and mascara…"

Solae had gone out with Hershel three times, twice with the boys, but as frazzled as she sounded, one would think this was her friend's first date. Candace laughed as she slipped into a long printed skirt and black top. "That's not the look I'm going for on a school night with my Lindsay…"

Candace strained her hearing. "What's that noise in the background?"

"Oh, girl, that's my EMS and fire scanners," she stated nonchalantly as if they were commercials between her favorite program.

"What? When did you buy those?" Candace frowned and stared at her phone. "Solae, why do—"

"Hi Aunt Sollie," her daughter shouted at the mention of her name as she raced into Candace's bedroom. With her comb and brush in hand, Lindsay flopped on the floor in front of Candace so she could touch up her ponytails.

"Okay, so when did you pick up this hobby?"

"Since Captain Hershel Kavanaugh."

"Hmmm." Candace was amused. *What silly thing will I pick up?*

"I just want to know he's safe when he's not with me. I told you to trust God, but I should take my own advice, right?"

Nodding, Candace was careful what she said in front of Lindsay. "So…does he know you have one?"

"Who do you think helped me pick it out?" Solae giggled. "He thought it was sweet and said he could get me an old one at the station. But I wanted a new one and refused his offer to buy it. If a man wants to buy me a gift, it's certainly not going to be an all-in-one medical/fire/police scanner."

With Lindsay's hair back in order, Candace sent her into the living room to watch television. "Since he confided in you about his marriage, have you told me about …you know?"

"Not yet." She sighed.

"I'm batting two for two when it comes to blowing a relationship. I thought I was safe with Eric and Charles, who both professed to love me. When I told them about the excruciating pain I suffered that led to a hysterectomy, there wasn't enough love to make them stick around."

When Solae paused, Candace could feel her friend's mental and emotional pain, neither of which healed after the procedure.

If Royce could want her with her little package, Candace prayed that Hershel or some other man would want Solae just as much, even if she couldn't have children.

"Don't give up. The same God that drew Royce to me when I wasn't looking is the same God that can send a wonderful Christian man to you. Hopefully it's Hershel. "

"I hope so, too," she said softly.

"This is a first for you in a relationship. Maybe it won't matter to Hershel, since he already has children." Candace searched for encouraging words. "Let's pray that it's God's will that Hershel's the one."

"Amen." Solae was quiet, then cleared her throat. "Anyway, we're going to the movies on his next night off. I could always casually mention, while my hand is in the popcorn bowl, that I can't have children."

Uh-oh. Solae is on the verge of a pity party.

Normally the two would talk out their issues—sometimes for hours—until one felt that the other friend was okay. Unfortunately, it was the first time in years that one of them wasn't available for a marathon conversation.

"Mommy!" Lindsay yelled from her room.

"Listen, I've got to go and finish getting ready—"

"Oh right, and here I am rambling on about myself. I hope I didn't spoil your mood. Have a good time."

"Wait. Let's pray first."

Closing her eyes, Candace heard Solae sniff as she petitioned God, "Father, in the mighty name of Jesus, my friend is hurting and I'm hurting for her. I know You love us and Your Word says that You desire that we would prosper and be in good health, even as our soul prospers in 3 John 1:2.

"Lord, we've been feeding our souls with Your Word; now I ask that You would bless my friend's life, whether it would be with Hershel or another man, but let the man who finds her, know he has found a good woman, in Jesus' name. Amen."

"Amen," Solae repeated followed by a couple of sniffs. "Thank you, sister. Now go have fun. Call me when you get back. Bye." After mustering up a chuckle, she disconnected.

Candace wasn't laughing as she thought about how much Solae could get hurt if Hershel wasn't sincere once she decided to open up about her condition.

It was hard for Candace to push aside her concern for her friend.

Cast all your cares upon Me, for I care for you, God spoke 1 Peter 5:7.

She meditated on that verse as she walked into her bathroom and reached for her makeup bag. As she dusted blush on her cheeks, she continued to talk to Jesus, "Lord, it's not just Solae who has concerns about a relationship; help me, too." When her doorbell buzzed, Candace jumped and glanced at the time. A minute late, but she would give him that.

"Mommy, someone's here." Lindsay yelled, running into her bedroom as if she couldn't hear the bell.

Candace checked her appearance and took a deep breath before being led away by Lindsay to the living room. Lindsay peeped from behind her as she opened the door.

"Mr. Fireman," Lindsay screamed and waved.

PAT SIMMONS

Royce's eyes twinkled as he crossed her threshold, forcing her to step back or risk his teasing her about a kiss. "For you." He handed her a flower that she noticed once she stopped looking at him.

"Thank you."

He squatted and gave Lindsay a flower, she looked up at Candace. "Tell him thank you."

She did and surprisingly, gave him a hug before retreating back behind her legs again.

"We're going to get something to eat." Lindsay babbled. "Do you want to go with us, Mr. Fireman?"

"I'm going to Chuck E. Cheese's. Wanna go with me?"

Lindsay's widened with eager anticipation. "Can we go with him, Mommy?"

"Yes, baby."

Royce seemed distracted as he performed a quick sweep of her ceilings. He smiled when he caught her staring at him. "Smoke detector." He pointed.

Stuffing his hands in his pockets, he shrugged. "Just making sure you're safe. Mind if I check them?"

"Go right ahead." Leaning against the wall, she folded her arms as she and Lindsay watched him in work mode.

"Did I pass?"

"Yes, madam." Royce escorted them out the door with Lindsay in between them, latched onto both their hands.

He listened patiently as Lindsay rambled on about her dolls, then her teacher and the little boy who always wanted to share his lunch. She and Royce exchanged a knowing glance.

At Chuck E. Cheese, Lindsay was a ball of energy. After deciding on what kind of pizza she wanted, Lindsay made a beeline for the play area.

102

"She's beautiful," Royce said as they chose a table in bird's eye view of her.

"Mommy, Mr. Fireman," Lindsay yelled from her perch on the slide.

"You're beautiful, too. Whatever you did to your hair really flatters your face. You are one pretty woman." His eyes seemed to have a mind of their own as they scanned her face.

Reaching for her hand, Candace was hesitant about relinquishing them, but she craved his touch. She could hear Solae's voice, coaxing her that it's okay to be wooed. Once her hand was secure in his grip, Royce began to play with her fingers. "You have a special little girl there."

"I know. Thank you. She's a ball of energy." When she faced him, it was hard to look into his mesmerizing eyes and not be drawn in. She lowered her lashes. "Thank you for listening to her nonstop chatter."

"Do you know how much I can learn about the mother from listening to the babblings of her child?" he asked with a serious tone, then laughed when she cast him one of her threatening looks. "But I'd rather learn those things from Mama Bear herself."

Candace checked on Lindsay again. One of her biggest fears as a parent was sexual predators, so as far as she was concerned, she couldn't watch her too carefully. Double checking that she was safely playing with another child, she turned back to Royce, who was watching her.

"What?"

Twisting his mouth, Royce looked away as their order was set in front of them. He thanked the woman. Bowing his head, he led them in a quick prayer. As soon as he said amen, he looked toward the play area for Lindsay.

"There are so many things I want to know about you, but I know our time is limited tonight," he admitted with a hint of frustration. "Why haven't you remarried?"

Lindsay reappeared as they were reaching for their first slice of pizza. She was out of breath when she flopped next to Candace.

"Wait." Pulling out a disinfectant wipe, she cleaned her daughter's hands. Royce seemed patient as she tended to Lindsay.

"Having fun?" he asked her.

"Yeah!" She bobbed her head.

As Lindsay chatted between bites and breaths, they both listened. Royce didn't seem annoyed by the third wheel on their first date.

Lindsay wiped her mouth after two slices of half eaten pizza. "Can I go back and play?"

Both set of eyes were on her as Candace checked her watch. Since the date included Lindsay, they didn't have much time left. "Five more minutes, then we have to go. It's Wednesday, a school night."

"Okay, Mommy." She raced off to Candace's relief. She wanted a few more minutes with Royce to be transported to a place where she was not just a mommy, but a woman who was eligible for the dating pool.

Chapter 17

Cuddling a sleeping Lindsay in his arms, Royce escorted Candace to her door. He sighed in frustration because he wasn't ready to say goodnight.

"Call me when you get home, okay?" Her request was soft just like her hands, which he'd held and caressed earlier.

"You don't have to ask me twice." He planted a kiss in her hair when he really wanted her lips.

Royce made sure they were safe inside, then handed over Lindsay. Quenching the urge for a hug, he did an about face and trekked back to his vehicle. One thing he didn't want to do was rush Candace without her willingness to commit her heart to a new relationship.

Although he drove the speed limit, Royce couldn't get home fast enough. Once he cleared his doorway, Royce punched her number in his phone.

He was smiling before she answered. Royce was about to get comfortable to talk as long as she wanted when something told him to turn around.

In his haste to get inside his home, he had left his car running with the door open in the driveway. Retracing his steps, Royce laughed at himself, not believing he had been so irresponsible. With his car off and keys in hand, he headed back to his house.

"I wish we'd had more face-to-face time tonight. Did I tell you how pretty you looked?" She was very youthful in her appearance. If Candace was wearing makeup, it was so faint, he could barely see it.

"You're not bad on the eyes either. I think every woman who came within one foot of us did a double take."

"I would like for us to become a couple, so that will take away the mystery of our status."

Candace was silent for a few moments. He wondered what she was thinking about his continued forwardness. "I would like for us to get to know each other better. Maybe the next time we go out, I can get a babysitter for Lindsay."

Yes, Royce pumped his fist in the air. Wiping the grin off his face as if she could see him, he schooled his tone. "Whatever makes you comfortable," he said to please her.

"What do you think about us double dating with your brother and Solae?"

He didn't. They were going from having her child as a chaperone to his big brother? *Unnecessary.* Royce groaned inwardly. Her hesitation about him seemed so foreign compared to the other two women he'd dated with children. They always tried to be a step ahead of him. They didn't want their children around at all.

"Okay, I'll talk to Hershel to see when we're both off together. That could be a week or more. I know I don't want to wait more than seven days to see you again."

"I'm cooking spaghetti and meatballs for dinner tomorrow… While I want to take this new relationship slow, I really don't want to wait that long either."

Thank you Jesus! "What time is dinner served?"

"About five-thirty."

"I'll be there at five-twenty to set the table if you want…and I'll bring a French loaf and a treat for Lindsay."

"You plan to bribe my baby?" she teased.

"Absolutely. I have no shame." Minutes later, Royce disconnected with a smile.

The next evening, Royce hummed as he shaved in preparation to have dinner with Candace and Lindsay. Next, he stretched a black turtle neck over his head and biceps. Instead of jeans, he chose black slacks. Noting the time, Royce hurried so he could pick up the French loaf, juice and cupcakes for Lindsay and a bouquet for Candace.

Half an hour later, Royce stood on her small porch, ringing her doorbell. He heard Lindsay's squeal of excitement before Candace opened the door. Her beauty had him tongue-tied. It took a few moments for him to recover. "Hi…for you." He handed her the flowers.

Lindsay stood on the sidelines, waiting for her goodies. Royce handed her a bag with a half dozen cupcakes. "Yay. Mr. Royce. Mommy, I got cupcakes," she said excitedly, leaving them to their own thoughts as she surveyed the icing.

After stepping inside, Royce handed her the other bag and shook off his jacket. He couldn't help scrutinizing her shapely figure outlined in a long sweater dress. It was a casualty of being one-hundred percent male, but he didn't allow his eyes to linger. That was the power of the Holy Ghost.

"Hmm. Something smells good." Royce glanced around, admiring again the décor that he had already seen. She was a master at blending colors he would never have imagined worked together.

"I hope you like my homemade sauce." Her eyes twinkled as she headed toward the kitchen that appeared, so far, to be the largest room in the small bungalow.

"I'm sure I will, or I'll acquire a taste for it."

She stopped and playfully nudged him. "Do you always say the right things?"

"Not always, but I've learned to speak from my heart."

"You're a fascinating man," she said over her shoulder as she turned off the stove and pointed to an overhead cabinet. "The plates are there. You can wash your hands in the sink."

He did as he was told before grabbing the three plates. Lindsay stood at his side eagerly waiting to help set the table. "I hope that works in my favor."

"It already has." Blushing, Candace placed the dish on the table that was loaded with simmering spaghetti and topped with a layer of Parmesan cheese.

Royce didn't know a salad could look so inviting with the green, red and yellow vegetables peeping from the serving bowl. Soon, they were gathered around her kitchen table. It was an impressive oak wood table for four. Too nice for a kitchen, but she used it for everyday purposes as if she wasn't concerned about a child's marks and dents.

Come to think of it, Candace's house was tastefully decorated with very little that hinted that a child lived there except for a few children's books or DVDs. She was neat—a good sign.

"Do you mind saying grace?"

"I don't," Royce told her as he reached for their hands. When Candace gently rested hers in his, he imagined that her gesture was a quiet admission that she was putting her trust in him. "Father, in the mighty name of Jesus, I thank You for the cross at Calvary. I thank You for this fellowship with two beautiful ladies." He paused when he heard Lindsay giggle. "Lord, please sanctify this food as You do our lives and bless it for our nourishment in Jesus' name."

They all said amen in unison.

The conversation during dinner was child-friendly, which he expected, but a few times he caught Candace's glances that let him know she wished for privacy.

After a second helping of everything, Royce pushed back from the table and patted his stomach. "That was good ba—" He caught himself.

"Thank you. It's good to know that at least one other person, besides Solae and Lindsay, appreciate my culinary skills."

"Yes, and to show my appreciation, you can invite me over any time after my thirty-hour shift has ended." Standing, Royce took the liberty of gathering his plate and hers while Lindsay played with the remains of her salad. "Do you want me to wash?"

She seemed surprised by his offer. "Why, thank you, but no, I have a dishwasher."

"Mommy, can I be excused and watch TV? I finished my homework."

"But I haven't checked it, baby."

"I'll do that," Royce said. He wanted to insinuate himself in their lives as a prerequisite to something more permanent. Candace was the one—he had no doubt about that—but he had to wait for her to come to the realization that he was more than her stepping stone back to the dating life.

"Oh, okay. Thank you again. Lindsay, go get your

folder, sweetie. When they were alone, she stepped closer. "I don't know where this is going between us, but don't play with my child." She lowered her voice even more, "Lindsay doesn't know anything about loss and she better not learn it from you."

The lioness with the fiery darts in her beautiful brown eyes issued her warning, but he had his own. "Then make yourself comfortable, Miss Clark, because I don't plan to lose."

Candace's steam seeped out as Lindsay ran back into the room. She retreated to the sink where she rinsed the dishes without saying another word. Great, maybe his honesty had worked against him this time. Although he checked Lindsay's schoolwork with care, his mind never stopped wondering what Candace could possibly be thinking.

His answer came less than an hour later when she walked him to the door. "I really like you and I'll admit that I'm attracted to you, but I can't go this fast…"

He folded his arms and stared. If she was about to end something before it started, then Royce wanted to make sure he steeled himself against the disappointment, so he could bounce back with more vigor to fight for what he wanted.

"I can't pray on this alone. I need you to pray right alongside me."

He liked the challenge in her eyes.

"I want you to slow down, but my heart likes the speed you're moving, so…" she paused. "If you're available Sunday morning, I would like to invite you to our church and maybe afterward you could join us for dinner."

That was asking a lot coming off a three day shift, but

Royce was going to make it work. "I'll get off Sunday at eight. I'll shower, dress and be here to get you and Lindsay by nine-thirty." It was going to be a long day, but Royce wanted her, so he had no problem proving his worth.

Chapter 18

"Turn on channel five," Solae said with urgency in her voice. "Quick."

Candace didn't as she continued to scan her closet for something to wear to church the following day. It would be the first time Royce would accompany her and Lindsay and she wanted to look her best. "Why?" Her friend could be so dramatic at times.

"They're talking about a huge fire in North County!"

Her friend had it bad. Candace shook her head. Since dating Hershel, she had definitely turned into a fire chaser. She owned two fire scanners because the first one didn't provide a large enough coverage.

Now Solae was hooked on anything about fires—TV shows, books, or movies. The woman seemed to sniff out smoke before the flames got going good. "Okay?"

"Engine House Eight is on the scene of a four alarm fire. More equipment is being requested…some firefighters have been injured!"

"What?" Candace's body froze as her heart pounded out of control. Now was a good time to be concerned. That was Royce and Hershel's firehouse.

She couldn't get out the closet fast enough to get to her television. She reached for the remote and clicked on the flat screen in the privacy of her bedroom.

It was a good thing Lindsay was in the living room, watching a cartoon show. Thank God she didn't allow Lindsay to watch the news.

Her daughter would probably be beside herself, like Candace was now, if she thought something happened to Mr. Royce.

The noise from Solae's scanner arsenal blared in her ear. Everything was so garbled up, Candace couldn't make out anything until a dispatcher's voice silenced the chaos, "All companies, evacuate the building. Structure unstable. Evacuate the building," the woman repeated it several times as if she was a recording.

Channel five captured the spectacular flames as the backdrop to a cloudless night sky. In the midst of the fireworks display, responders began carrying out three firefighters. None of them were walking on their own.

"Are you seeing it?"

With her jaw dropped, Candace stared. She had forgotten that Solae was even on the phone.

She felt light-headed as paramedics began to pull off the head gear and administered oxygen to the injured firefighters. "Why don't the cameramen zoom in closer!" She needed to see and make sure Royce wasn't hurt.

Everything seemed to move in slow motion as medics began to load the firefighters into waiting ambulances. Patting her chest, Candace held her breath. "Lord, please let Roy…" That would be so selfish. "Jesus, save them and comfort their families. Please let them be okay, in Jesus' name. Amen," she said in a whisper, but Solae seconded the amen.

"Mommy, can I have a snack?" Lindsay asked from the other side of her closed door.

Racing to the door to keep Lindsay from coming in, Candace answered, "Ah, sure baby. One snack," she said to get rid of her. Otherwise, there was no way she would allow her daughter a snack so close to bedtime.

Her knees weakened as she sank onto the edge of the bed, hoping she judged the distance to catch her weight, or her bottom would land on the floor.

Between the dispatchers instructing police to block streets along the ambulance routes to the hospitals, and video from the station's chopper capturing the urgency, Candace was overwhelmed. "I can't watch this."

"I know...hold on. Hershel's calling me on my cell. Hello?" Solae voice faded. Seconds later, she gasped.

"What?" Candace tried to get her friend's attention. "Solae!"

Solae sniffed. "Okay. Keep me posted," she said on the other line, then was silent. "What? What's wrong? Is it—"

"I'm on my way. Royce has been injured."

Candace willed herself to stay composed and not lose it, at least until Solae got there. "Okay," she remembered saying. She withheld her sobs and silently mourned for the unknown. "Lord, not again."

She thought about Daniel and all they had meant to each other in their short marriage and then Royce and what could have been.

Ask in My name and I will do it, God spoke John 14:13.

Sliding to her knees, Candace moaned and mumbled her requests. When she was no longer able to form her words, an explosion of tongues escaped her mouth until she submitted to the Holy Ghost to speak intercessory prayer for the injured firefighters.

Soon, she felt Lindsay at her side praying in her innocent childish way, not knowing her anguish. But her presence was comforting.

Candace's spirit began to quiet minutes before her doorbell rang.

"Mommy, doorbell." Lindsay tapped her shoulder.

"Thank You, Jesus for what You're going to do, in Jesus' name. Amen," she finished before getting to her feet and following her daughter out her bedroom.

Seconds after opening her door, Candace fell into Solae's arms. Mindful of her daughter, she held her tears at bay.

"Aunt Sollie, you want to see the picture I colored?" Lindsay asked.

"Sure baby, let me talk to your mommy first, okay? How about you color three more pictures for me to hang on my refrigerator?"

"Yeah. Okay." She raced off to do her godmother's bidding.

Candace dragged Solae to her bedroom. Once they were behind closed doors, she impatiently waited for an update. "What did Hershel say? Is Royce...is he alive? Is he going to be okay?"

Solae *shh*ed her with her hand and guided her to her bed to sit. "Hershel called me while I was on the way here. He told me to tell you that Royce is okay. None of the firefighters' injuries are critical."

"What does okay mean?" Candace snapped. "What hospital is he in? I need to see him for myself."

She was working herself into a mental frenzy until she grasped hold on one of Solae's soft prayers. Her spirit relaxed and she began to pray again.

"I need to go see him, Solae."

"You will, but not tonight. You can't drive in this mental state, and I can't drive you because we'll have to take Lindsay along and she doesn't need to see this. I'm spending the night and in the morning you can go to Barnes Hospital while I stay here."

At least it's not the same hospital where Daniel died. Hopefully that was a good sign.

Lord, please let me be that praying woman that Royce needs right now. "I don't know how much sleep I'm going to get."

"I know, but we've got to trust God on this." Solae advised.

"You're right. This can't be about my insecurities right now," Candace said, staring at nothing. "This is about Royce." She stood to get Lindsay ready for bed and to try to get some sleep herself; but come daylight, even without an alarm clock, she would be dressed and en route to the hospital.

It seemed as if Candace had spent all night praying instead of sleeping. She showered and put on the first skirt and sweater off the rack. Since makeup couldn't hide the puffiness under her eyes, Candace didn't bother.

The quiet thirty minute drive into the city gave Candace time to think whether or not she wanted to be in a relationship that would probably give her many more restless nights like the previous one.

By the time she reached the hospital's parking garage, she still didn't have an answer.

With her pocket Bible and small bottle containing Holy Oil, she got out of her car and willed her legs to be steady as she left the garage and walked through the hospital's entrance.

She stopped at the information desk and asked for Royce's room number.

Taking the elevators to the fourth floor, Candace prayed silently, not knowing what to expect. Hershel said he was okay, but a person with broken bones and bruised ribs could be considered okay, too.

As her heart pounded she forced herself to get out of the elevator. She noted each room number as she walked closer to her destination.

Stopping in front of room 437, Candace tapped softly on the door that was ajar before proceeding. When she caught sight of the IV and the monitor, her eyes welled up with tears, blurring her vision as she glanced at the sleeping figure in the bed. *Sleeping or unconscious?*

The man who always seemed strong and powerful lay quietly with a large bandage on his head. Despite his brown skin, she noticed several abrasions and deep purple bruises on one cheek and another on his right shoulder.

Royce must have sensed her presence because his eyes fluttered open. He gave her a smile that reached his eyes before his hand beckoned her closer.

Those threatening tears began to stream down her face. "I said I wasn't going to cry." She dabbed at her eyes before digging into the bottom of her purse for tissue. She pulled a few out as well as the Holy Oil.

After squeezing sanitizer into her hands, she clasped

his. Royce's squeeze was so strong that she couldn't help but smile. "I was so worried about you."

"Sorry, baby."

The first time he called her that, Royce had mumbled it in his sleep. The second time, he let it slip and she silently questioned it. Now, the endearment gave Candace contentment.

Swallowing, she eyed the bandage on his head. "I've been praying since I heard the news." She unscrewed the cap and tilted the bottle on her finger. When she dabbed the oil on his forehead, Royce closed his eyes.

She followed suit and then bowed her head. Her voice wavered in the beginning, but gained strength as she remembered what her God could do. "Lord, in the mighty name of Jesus, I thank You for protecting Royce and the others. I thank You for the precious blood shed for our sins. Thank You, God, for increasing my faith in You. I ask that You command and breathe on his body Your healing power, in Jesus' name. Amen."

Before she could open her eyes, Royce made an addendum to her prayer. "Jesus, thank You for placing Candace and Lindsay in my life. I know You have a blessing for your servants, a crossing guard and a firefighter and I thank You in advance, in Jesus' name. Amen."

"Amen," she whispered again. She reached out to tenderly stroke his jaw. She hoped her touch would be soothing. "Thank you." He pulled her hand to his mouth and brushed a kiss there, which made her fingers tingle.

"How do you feel?" she asked, noting he looked as tired as she felt from lack of a good night's sleep.

"My head still hurts, but I'm alive. When I noticed the second floor begin to cave in above me, I saw that my comrade was still up there. I tried to reach Allen, but he was standing right on the spot where the floor gave way.

"I was knocked unconscious by falling debris. My x-rays and CAT scan came back normal, so I'll probably be released today, thank You, Jesus. Allen has a bruised shoulder. Another firefighter suffered minor smoke inhalation."

He paused, noticing her steady stream of tears. He used the thumb of his other hand to gently wipe them away. "There will always be the possibility of danger and uncertainty associated with my job. Think you can you handle it?"

"I've been asking myself the same question as I drove here."

"And the answer is…?"

She was slow in responding. Whatever came out of her lips, she had to mean it from the depths of her heart. "I want to try," Candace finally admitted. "The rational side of me is saying, 'Are you crazy to take this on after losing a loved one the first time, but I'm starting to understand your drive to live each day as if it's your last."

Out of nowhere a yawn escaped. Candace tried to cover it with her free hand; she couldn't. Another one was on its heels.

Candace glanced at Royce who had suddenly dozed off. She smiled. *Thank You, Jesus, he's okay.* Wiggling in the recliner next to his bed, searching for a comfortable position, she closed her eyes and drifted off with their hands still linked. She couldn't let go, and apparently, neither could he.

Chapter 19

Royce had no complaints during his convalescence at home following his discharge. Candace had cooked a week's worth of dinners and delivered them to his doorstep.

As a way to prolong their visits, he began to play a game, of sorts, with Lindsay, drilling her about fire safety. Her reward would always be stickers of some kind, which she loved.

"Mommy and I brought you a stuffed animal, Mr. Royce, so you'll get better," Lindsay had explained during a short visit. He gave her a hug and then looked into the eyes of her beautiful mother. *"I love her, Jesus. Now, please let her love me back."*

True to his word, a week after he had returned to work, he scheduled on his upcoming off day a double date with Hershel and Solae at Kobe Steakhouse. He hadn't forgotten the request she'd made before his accident.

Even though they would be with his brother and her friend, it would be their first real date without a child chaperone.

Candace dressed carefully for her date under her daughter's watchful eye.

"You look pretty, Mommy," Lindsay complimented from her stretched-out position on Candace's bed.

"Thank you, sweetie." Candace studied herself in the mirror, checking the view front and back of the mid-sleeve, knee length, black knit dress that stretched with her curves.

Since Royce had commented more than once about her legs, she slipped into higher heels that Solae would classify as stilettoes to give her added height. She swept up her curls and allowed a few strands to dangle. She was ready by the time her doorbell buzzed.

Lindsay leaped off her bed and scrambled to the door where she waited impatiently for Candace to come and open it. As if it was her first time meeting Royce Kavanaugh, her heart fluttered.

His nostrils flared as he came within inches of her face, stepping into her house.

"Wow." He whistled, bringing her to mind the first time he had whistled at her on her first day as a crossing guard. "You look beautiful."

"What about me, Mr. Royce," Lindsay interrupted their private moment, vying for his attention.

Lifting her into his arms, he tickled her. "You always look like a princess."

Lindsay rewarded him with a tight hug before he stood her on her feet. The doorbell buzzed again and it was an elderly neighbor who Candace trusted to babysit her angel.

After Candace received her hugs and kisses from

Lindsay, they said their goodbyes.

While en route, Candace closed her eyes so she could enjoy the moment; the instrumental gospel jazz coming from the car speakers, the woodsy scent of his cologne and the long masculine fingers that were linked with hers.

The comfort Royce brought her made her realize the affection she had been missing.

"Thank you," she mumbled without opening her eyes.

"For what?"

"Convincing me that happiness could still exist."

He brought her hand to his mouth and brushed his lips against her fingers. She fluttered her lids open and they both stared at each other. "Thank you for saying yes and for taking care of me."

"I would do it again," she said sincerely.

"And I will try never to put you in a situation that would require you to do that again. Although I would have to repent if I said I haven't enjoyed your and Lindsay's tender loving care."

His words made Candace shiver, then she smiled.

Soon, they arrived at West Port Plaza where Royce parked and then helped her out. Reaching for her hand, Candace accepted his secure hold as they strolled toward Kobe Steakhouse.

Solae and Hershel were already in the lobby waiting for them.

Wearing the same shade of brown, the pair complemented each other as their eyes seemed to dance with happiness. She sensed that Solae had finally found the right one.

The ladies hugged, the gentlemen shook hands and then rode the elevator to the top floor that housed the restaurant. Almost immediately, the couples were led to a room where others were camped out at a table, facing their chef.

Taking the four empty seats to complete the group, the chef began his theatrics. She and Royce would occasionally slip into their own world with smiles and touches. She was falling hard for him.

She and Solae giggled at the brothers' attempts at catching with their mouths chunks of meat that the chef would playfully flip their way from the grill. It was hilarious.

Their server poured several different sauces into the small ramekins at each place setting. Candace wrinkled her nose at the pungent smell, but Royce scooped up a bit on his spoon, leaned closer, and coaxed her to sample the ginger sauce. Trusting him, she closed her eyes and sampled just enough to catch a hint of its favor. The taste was just as strong as it odor.

"How about this?" He brushed his soft lips against hers.

Her eyes widened in surprise. That was their first kiss—per se—and in public at that. She blushed, glancing around to see who else had witnessed their moment. But the other six couples appeared occupied with conversation or eating. Even Solae wasn't looking her way.

"I like that flavor," she whispered as she looked at him through the hooded shade of her lashes. "It has a lingering sweetness to it."

Royce winked as their chef clanked his utensils on the grill. "It's good to know my lady has a sweet tooth." With a lopsided grin, Royce pulled back. "Having a good time, babe?"

"I like hearing you call me that." Indeed, she felt like a modern day Cinderella. "Yes, I am. Thank you." She nudged his shoulder.

"I aim to please, *Miss Clark*, babe."

The evening progressed with group discussions of one another's relationship status, married, single, or engaged.

Royce hung his arm on the back of her chair and stared into Candace's eyes while answering the question. "We're both single *for now*."

Next, the topic of professions floated among them.

"A firefighter and a captain...wow." A pretty woman gave Hershel and Royce a dreamy expression. Candace recognized the hero worship. Her daughter wore it every time Royce came to visit.

Evidently, the woman's companion noticed her gaze and switched the subject to the improving economy.

Half-listening, Candace reached into her purse for her cell phone to check in with her babysitter.

Royce craned his neck to see the message she was typing. "Is everything okay?" She appreciated his concern for her child. Within minutes, Sister Finney texted back.

Yur baby and I watching the Lion King for 2 times. She'll be sleep when u come.

Candace snickered. The woman was still getting the hang of texting.

The festive evening ended too soon as they tipped the chef and prepared to leave. Lost in their own worlds, it seemed as if Candace and Solae had forgotten about each other. Royce pulled back Candace's chair and helped her to her feet, then snaked his arm around her waist.

The couples left together. Outside in the parking lot, the moon cast a spotlight on them. As the women hugged,

Candace whispered, "Happy?"

"I'm in love." Solae gave her the smile that made her favor Nia Long.

Me, too, Candace mouthed as Royce separated them and escorted her to his vehicle. *I'm in love again*, Candace digested the words. Love had actually captured her by surprised. Embracing the utopia, Candace broke free of Royce's hand and ran to the car, laughing with happiness. Royce gave chase and scooped her off her feet. Before she landed, they shared their first *real* kiss. "I'm in love with you, Miss Clark."

Her vision blurred as she choked out her answer. "I love you, too."

Chapter 20

Candace squealed when a bouquet of flowers was delivered to her desk.

"Mine is bigger," Solae good-naturedly teased. Hershel had sent her flowers earlier in the week. Her friend knew how to pamper them in such a way that they always looked fresh.

Ignoring the dig, Candace closed her eyes and indulged in a slow cleansing whiff of the scent, then slowly exhaled. She couldn't wait for his shift to end so she and Lindsay could see him again.

Moments later, she wheeled her chair to Solae's workstation and anchored her elbows on the desk. With a slight pout, she eyed her friend. "I assume you'll be seeing Mr. Kavanaugh soon. Sixteen hours and twenty minutes before Royce is off. Actually, I better tack on another ten hours for him to catch up on his sleep once he gets home."

Candace bit her bottom lip. "I don't want to wait that long to see him. I was thinking Lindsay and I could pay Royce a surprise visit at the station with a hot meal."

"Work your plan, girl."

The day sped by until it was time to leave for her

crossing guard duty. Once she and Lindsay got home, she started preparing a beef stew for dinner with enough to take to the station. Actually, Candace cleaned up the mess as Lindsay chatted away. "Mommy, I love Mr. Royce."

Her declaration didn't surprise Candace as gave Lindsay a tender smile. "Me, too."

"Do you think he loves me?" She looked up with a hopeful expression from working a word puzzle assigned as her homework.

"Yes, sweetie. I think Mr. Royce especially loves children because he likes to save them." Candace wanted to be careful in her response. Royce was making it too easy for her and Lindsay to become attached to his presence. He hadn't offered them permanency.

Although she wasn't opposed to that next step, she didn't know how soon she would be ready, but that didn't stop her feelings from growing.

"Since my daddy is with Jesus, I'm going to ask God to make Mr. Royce my daddy," the five year old said matter-of-factly.

Oh boy. Candace swallowed. "Lindsay, whenever we ask God for something, we're to say, 'Lord, if this is Your will', remember?" She nodded to prompt her daughter.

"Yep, but God loves me and He wants me to have a daddy."

Really? Candace left it at that as she added a bit of seasoning to the pre-cooked beef. God would definitely have the last word on that.

Once the stew was ready and the store-bought rolls Lindsay had placed on the cookie sheet were done, she carefully boxed everything up.

"I like going to the firehouse, Mommy," she said as

Candace bundled her up before handing her the bag of warm rolls.

En route, Candace selfishly prayed there wouldn't be a fire or other medical emergency before she and Lindsay got there.

Engine House Eight was one of the many newer fire stations that had been built in the last couple of years throughout North County.

She had seen the majestic structure that reminded her of a boutique hotel many times in passing. Candace never would have guessed that she would one day be attracted to a firefighter that resided inside. Exactly thirteen minutes later, she turned into the parking lot and pulled into a spot on the side.

"Yay! Do you think Mr. Royce will let me see the fire truck?" Her eyes were wide with excitement.

"I don't know, baby. Maybe, if he's not busy." Before getting out her car, she sent Royce a text: I'm outside, can you let me in? C

Steadying the pot in her arms, Candace walked cautiously to the massive front door with Lindsay trailing her. A blast of cold air made her pause. Royce was already barreling out the door, zipping up his jacket as he headed their way.

"Hey, baby." He kissed her hair, something he did when Lindsay was around. His lips curled into a sexy smirk. "I like surprises, especially beautiful ones."

Candace blushed when he relieved her of the pot, then took Lindsay's package before bestowing a kiss on her hat-covered head. Her daughter beamed.

Royce ushered them inside the building and straight to the kitchen. After placing the items on the table, he helped

Candace shrug off her coat. Lindsay waited patiently for her turn for him to assist her with her cap, gloves and coat.

"I've missed you. I know it's only been two days, but I still missed you." He warmed her ear with another hidden kiss.

"That's why we're here. We've missed you, too."

"Me, too." Lindsay grinned, boasting a gap left by a recent missing tooth.

"I was hoping you would be hungry, so Lindsay and I made a beef stew..."

Rubbing his abs, he towered over her head, staring. "I'm famished."

"If you have time to eat now, wash your hands. Show me where the bowls are and I'll fix it. If not, you can have it later."

"If I eat now, will you stay?" Royce lifted the lid. He closed his eyes as he inhaled.

"Just for a little while. I need to get Lindsay home and in bed.

The aroma must have sounded a silent alarm as two firefighters peeped into the kitchen. "Did someone mention food?"

They laughed and Royce made the introductions before Candace explained, "There's enough food for ten hungry men."

That seemed to be a cue as almost that many came from out of nowhere and filed into the kitchen. Royce was the first to scoop the stew out the pot and grab a few rolls.

Sitting next to Royce, she was amused at the sounds of slurping and smacking around her while devouring her food. Lindsay was content to color until Royce was finished so he could show her the fire truck.

Twenty minutes later, she had to pull Lindsay away from the big engine. With the kitchen restored and the leftovers put up, it was time to go.

Lindsay gave him a quick hug goodbye, Candace lingered a little longer in his arms for hers. "I'll be praying for a peaceful and safe night," she whispered.

"Be safe, baby, and call me when you get home," he ordered.

She did just that when she walked through her door. Suddenly, sirens sounded in the background. Royce disconnected, barely saying goodbye.

Shaking her head, Candace smiled. Only Royce Kavanaugh could get away with hanging up on her. "Lord, keep him safe, in Jesus' name. Amen."

Chapter 21

"Have I told you I love you today?" Royce whispered into Candace's ear as they, including Lindsay, exited the Regal Theater at the St. Louis Outlet Mall.

Giggling like a school girl, she mouthed, *Every day.*

He winked. "Good, then I guess I'm doing my job."

Who said a man couldn't keep track of how long he had been dating a woman? Royce happily calculated that he had been taken off the market for two months and one week.

They were all dressed alike in their denim. He glanced down at Lindsay who was latched onto his other hand. "Did you enjoy the movie?"

With nothing less than worshipping eyes, she bobbed her head and then began to give him a recap of The Little Mermaid in 3D. "Hmmm-mm, did you see…"

Candace gave him one of those looks as if to say, 'You asked for it.'

Lifting Lindsay in his arms, Royce carried her to the food court to grab a bite to eat before spending the rest of the day at Candace's house doing absolutely nothing.

"Do you have plans for Thanksgiving?" she asked as he brought their trays with Subway sandwiches to the table.

Having Thanksgiving off came with a price. He was stuck working four twelve-hour shifts the day after. "It all depends. Things are always subject to change. Whenever our schedule permits, Hershel and I celebrate the holiday at Trent and Julia's home after we all attend morning church service. Do you and Lindsay have some sort of tradition?"

"We usually go to Solae's mom's house." She shrugged.

"Be my guest at my brother and sister-in-law's house," he stated. "I'm sure Hershel is bringing Solae."

"You know you have a bad habit of inviting folks to other folks' parties?"

Royce knew she was referring to his personal invitation for her to stay at his nephew's birthday party. "And I would do it again. Don't get me wrong, I love my nephew, but you were my focus. Please come." Pulling out his smartphone, he punched in Trent's number. "I'm bringing a guest for Thanksgiving."

"I'm not surprised." Trent snickered. "Candace and her daughter are more than welcome."

"Great." He disconnected seconds later and smiled. "See, you're invited."

Shaking her head, Candace chuckled. "That didn't sound like an invitation to me, but rather an order. I hope your sister-in-law won't mind, and I'll bring a dish."

"Julia won't." She was ecstatic when she got wind that he and Candace were a couple.

So a few weeks later, Candace and Lindsay accompanied Royce and Hershel to their church for Thanksgiving Day morning service. The choir sang a rendition of the old Walter Hawkins hit "Thank you."

Once the congregation's high praise ended, Pastor Reed preached his sermon. "As we celebrate Thanksgiving today, examine yourself. You should be so content in your present state that nothing more would add to your happiness. Your heart and mind should be convinced that you have what you need right in front of you. If you stay committed to Jesus, He'll add to your happiness without you asking for it…"

Royce couldn't help but think about the woman sitting near him, with only Lindsay separating them. He was actually in a contented place. His mind began to drift until Pastor Reed closed his Bible.

"Will you come today?" his pastor asked the visitors. "God's mercies are new every morning. Be thankful in your heart for another chance to repent and to get your sins washed away in Jesus' name. God will equip you with the Holy Ghost to live right. Won't you come?" Three people heeded his call for repentance. Ministers prayed for them while another prepared for the baptism that two of them had requested.

Standing with the rest of the congregation, Royce reached for Candace's hand as her eyes watered.

"This is the best part of the service. That's one less soul the devil has control over." Candace dabbed her eyes, witnessing two women be submerged spiritually dirty, then brought up gleaming sin free—redeemed.

Following the benediction, Royce and Hershel introduced the ladies to a few church members before heading to Trent and Julia's house with Candace's dish of potato salad and homemade rolls.

Hershel wasn't too far behind with the boys and Solae.

His brother had raved about Solae's desserts, so she brought sweet potato and pecan pies. Royce's mouth watered. This was one Thanksgiving he would never forget.

"Welcome," Julia met them at the door. Her eyes sparkled as she swallowed up Candace and Lindsay in hugs, then winked at Royce. As an afterthought, she gave him a hug. Minutes later, Julia repeated her routine with Solae.

Julia banished the Kavanaugh brothers to the family room to babysit the children. That translated to them watching a football bowl game on TV. When Trent's baby fussed, he gathered Ariel in his arms. That caused Lindsay to sit next to Royce to play with her. Royce smiled.

It was so natural between him and Lindsay. Strangers assumed they were father and daughter whenever they went into a restaurant or store, and he didn't have a problem accepting that role.

Soon the aromas from the kitchen made Royce's stomach growl while he strained to overhear the women's conversation. Losing interest in the game, Royce angled his body to have an unobstructed view of the kitchen to match Hershel's stare. He began to stroke his jaw in thought. "Are you thinking the same thing I'm thinking?" he asked Hershel without taking his eyes off Candace.

"What are *you* thinking?" Hershel countered.

He lowered his voice. "Thinking that it's time to ask the most beautiful woman in there to marry me."

"Solae is taken." Hershel didn't crack a smile. They stared at each other. Royce had wondered if his brother would ever allow another woman into life, not to mention in his heart again. Royce had his answer.

"You know I was referring to Candace. I think I'm ready."

"Me, too," Hershel stated casually, as if he was about to purchase the same pair of socks Royce wanted, and just that quickly he turned his attention back to the game.

Chapter 22

Candace and Solae were sitting side by side in the same pew they had occupied on Sundays for years while Sister Vanhorn read the morning announcements. From the upcoming fundraiser to choir rehearsal, nothing was sticking.

Memories from spending Thanksgiving Day with Royce from the church service, to the good night kiss at her door, to the whispers of 'I love you' when he got home, saturated her mind, then Royce's text that awaited her when she woke was on instant replay in her head.

Can't sleep thinking about you and me—and Lindsay. I love you and miss you so much. I think we should do something about it. Pray for me at church. Love R

"What did Sister Vanhorn say about the Christmas play?"

"Huh?" Candace blinked and stared at Solae. "Girl, I have no idea. My mind was elsewhere." She grinned sheepishly.

"Mine, too, but when she said something about the Christmas play, I thought about Hershel's boys."

Candace smiled, then chuckled. "Did you know

Brandon became protective of Lindsay at school when a classmate was picking on her?"

Solae snickered. "The big brother Lindsay never had."

"Yeah," Candace said softly. Lindsay would be an only child if she didn't remarry. Years ago she wouldn't have entertained that notion...now in love with Royce and his cryptic text message about "doing something" she didn't want to assume he meant a permanent spot in her life. After all, they hadn't been dating long.

As Sister Vanhorn continued to run through the church announcements in her monotone voice, Solae stared ahead, but mumbled, "Lately, I've been feeling Hershel watching me, and when I catch him, he just smiles."

"And the problem with that is?" Candace teased.

"Oh, what I wouldn't give to know his thoughts," Solae said, a tad frustrated.

"Well, one, he's attracted to you. Two, he does love you—"

Shaking her curls, Solae didn't wait for her to make it to number three. "Will he ask me to marry him? Especially since..." She scooted closer to Candace and whispered, "I told him about my inability to bear children."

Holding her breath, Candace swallowed. "What did he say?"

"He said it didn't matter."

Candace exhaled and squeezed Solae's hand. "Then believe him. You said yourself that Hershel is completely different from the others. Maybe it's because he's already a father."

"Please govern yourselves accordingly and make note of the changes for this week's services," Sister Vanhorn stated and stepped down from the pulpit.

Candace and Solae exchanged bewildered glances. "What changes?"

Missing the important stuff, it was as if God said, "That's what you get for talking when you should have been listening in My house."

Chapter 23

Just because, was Royce's reasoning for surprising Candace with flowers this morning. Although he was off and they were to have dinner later, Royce couldn't wait to see her.

He had calculated to be at her crosswalk about the same time the last school bell rang. Royce grinned, imagining her smile. He was almost there when the traffic snarled.

"Come on." People were messing with his agenda now.

Moments later, sirens grew louder as an emergency vehicle whizzed by him. Like the other drivers, Royce cranked his neck to see what was going on. That's when he noticed a news chopper hovering about three blocks in the distance.

Royce experienced a sinking feeling in his chest. He wondered if the source of the chaos was near Brandon's school and Candace's crosswalk. Swallowing back his emotions, Royce refused to believe the worst.

"Fine time to be off duty," he griped as another driver watched him talk to himself. Otherwise, he and his crew would be working the scene.

He clicked on the radio for a traffic report. "Police are on the scene of three car crash involving a school bus at the intersection of North Lindbergh and Cougar Lane. There are reports of injuries. You might want to avoid that area…"

"I don't think so!" Royce grunted as he performed a one second head check, then activated his blinker as a courtesy, but swerved into the right lane as if he'd been a race car driver in another life.

He inched his way forward until he could cut into a nearby Denny's parking lot. Royce scrambled out the car and started running toward the scene, praying, hoping that everyone would be all right and Candace wasn't involved.

Despite being in shape, Royce panted as his adrenaline propelled him faster. His fellow medics were tending to someone on a stretcher and another person's legs dangled from the back bumper of an ambulance— Candace! He would recognize those legs anywhere.

He bypassed colleagues with his mind set on the person in the back of the ambulance. Candace seemed fine as she sat still while the blood pressure cuff was being removed from her arm.

Looking up, she saw him and waved. The smile she graced him with caused him some ease—some.

"Baby, are you okay? What happened?" Royce gently patted her shoulder while frantic with questions.

"I'm fine, but the driver of the school bus is probably going to need a doctor and lawyer. Thank God no children were on board."

Nothing was making sense. "So…you're okay? I mean, I know how these accidents affect you," he said carefully.

Candace reached out and stroked his jaw. Now who

was comforting who? "Shaken up a little, but okay. I've learned that when God called me to do this job, He worked with the little faith I had and increased it, so I could be the best crossing guard possible."

"Uh-huh." That sounded good and he enjoyed testimonies like any other saint of God, but he needed answers. Royce turned to the medic who he recognized. "What happened, Jackson?"

"Witnesses say the bus driver ran the light, hitting two cars that were already in the intersection, including Miss Clark's, here." The smile Jackson gave his woman was too friendly in Royce's opinion.

"And…" Royce prompted, making a show of linking his fingers through Candace's hand.

Jackson noticed. "Apparently, the children had just been dropped off. The driver was arguing on the phone while attempting to drink hot coffee and drive, a bad combination. He has burns and probably has a concussion from jamming on the brakes and hitting his head against the windshield…"

"Now, are you okay?" Candace flipped the tables on him. She looked concerned.

Royce seemed to exhale for the first time. "No, I probably need them to check my blood pressure. I almost had a heart attack, thinking something bad happened."

Relieved that everything was okay, Royce wanted to collapse. Knowing he was much too heavy for Candace to catch his fall, he scooted her over instead and reached for the blood pressure cuff.

Candace had never seen Royce so beside himself. At least he had recovered from that morning's fiasco. However, since he picked her up for dinner an hour ago, Royce hadn't let go of her hand and she wasn't complaining.

As they stared at each other across the table, the candlelit setting played on all the love he had for her that shone from his eyes.

"I'm fine, sweetie," she tried to convince him. "You respond to emergencies all the time, so why don't you believe me?"

Royce shook his head. "I consider myself fearless; I have to be in order to do my job, but I've never been so scared in all my life. I thought I had lost you or that you were injured..." he looked away and swallowed.

At that moment, Candace knew he understood what it felt like to lose someone you love. After squeezing his fingers, she brought his knuckles to her lips.

"I love you, Mr. Kavanaugh. You once told me that in this life, nothing is for certain and that I should live each day as if were my last. I'm fine. I'm sorry for the scare, but let's enjoy the moment and our love."

"I can definitely do that." Clearing his throat, he waved for their waiter. "I guess I've worked up an appetite."

Chapter 26

Candace and Royce were about to have their first petty argument on Christmas Day. "Mr. Kavanaugh, you've got to be exhausted. Solae has turned me into a fire junkie. I watched last night's news about that building fire that took hours to put out."

Despite a horrific twelve hour shift that Royce worked on Christmas Eve, he insisted on accompanying Candace to church on Christmas Day and spending time with her and Lindsay.

"Thank God no one was injured, and that it wasn't a house fire where gifts were destroyed. Those are the most heart-wrenching incidents near the holidays." Royce made a stretching sound.

"I can hear the tiredness in your voice," she argued to no avail as he informed her he would be at her house in an hour.

"Be ready, *Miss* Clark."

"You are one stubborn man, but I love you. Merry Christmas."

"And my love for you is just as stubborn, babe. See you in fifty-nine minutes and Merry Christmas."

She gasped as he disconnected. Most times his persistence was attractive.

At the moment, it was frustrating her because he didn't give much time for her and Lindsay to get dressed.

At least they had taken their baths the previous night and laid out their clothes.

First, she would have to tangle with Lindsay to put away two of the five Christmas gifts she had already opened, which was her limit and it had nothing to do with her budget.

Her pastor reminded the congregation each year that Christmas was about celebrating Jesus' birthday, not anyone else's, and that God's offering should outmatch other's presents. That point hit home.

She dressed Lindsay in a dark green velvet dress with a satin bow tied in the back with green satin shoes. Her daughter primped in front of the wall length mirror as she twirled and danced from side to side.

With ten minutes and counting, Candace hurried and piled her mass of curls on top of her head and applied light makeup, then slipped into a red suede dress.

"You look pretty like me, Mommy."

"Thank you, sweetie," Candace said as she eyed her reflection in the same mirror temporarily vacated by her daughter.

The dress outlined her figure; her legs were hidden in suede knee boots.

Royce's face came alive when she opened the door not long after that. "Wow, woman." He stepped into her foyer carrying gifts, but couldn't seem to take his eyes off of her. Only Lindsay's piercing scream of delight at seeing him broke their connection.

"Hi, baby," he greeted Candace with love in his eyes, lowering his voice before Lindsay threw herself at him.

The moment was heartwarming as Candace freed him of the presents, so he could lift Lindsay into his arms. He gave her his full attention. "Don't you look like a princess?"

Lindsay nodded her head in agreement. Royce and Candace laughed as he graced them both with a kiss.

"We can open gifts after service," Candace informed Lindsay as she eyed the packages Royce brought. As expected her daughter pouted.

Seemingly taking pity on her sulking daughter, Royce tickled Lindsay, then made a production of bundling Lindsay up to her giggles. "I love you, Mr. Royce."

"And I love you, too." He capped off his declaration with a juicy smack on each cheek. "You're next." He turned to Candace and gave her the same treatment, bundling her up in her coat.

His tired eyes seemed to take on new life when he delivered several juicy smacks to her cheeks, nose, and forehead, purposely teasing her, leaving her lips untouched. Candace withheld her own pout.

As tit-for-tat, she planned to send him home packing soon after they returned from service, ate, and opened their gifts. En route to church, Lindsay led them in a round of familiar Christmas carols.

Twenty minutes later, they strolled into Jesus Saves Church as if they were a family. Locating a pew, they knelt and offered a prayer of thanks, almost in unison before taking their seats.

Once their coats were off, Candace snuggled as close as possible to Royce with Lindsay sandwiched between them.

Lord, thank You for the good man You allowed to find me, she said silently.

You had to overcome your fears in order for your blessings to find you, Jesus whispered in the wind.

Yes, I did. Candace smiled, grateful for that moment of fellowship with the Lord.

"What's so funny?" he whispered.

She hadn't realized Royce was watching her. "You make me smile for no reason at all."

It appeared her explanation brought out the cockiness in him as his lips curled into a smirk. Before he could respond, her pastor began his sermon. They both scrambled to flip through the pages of their Bibles, but he started without selecting a text.

"This is the day most of us have been waiting for, so today, it's time. God wants you to unwrap your gift," Pastor Alexander told the congregation.

"And guess what you'll find…Jesus revealed."

Candace jotted down the sermon title in her Bible.

"There is no guessing. After unwrapping Grace, we discover Mercy. Joy escaped and danced behind Peace. Salvation and Power stood at attention before Healing and Deliverance was uncovered. Somehow Love seemed to be a small package, but once opened, it exploded, covering all the other gifts."

Pastor Alexander quoted scriptures verbatim, faster than Candace could write, so she stopped. She would purchase the DVD.

Everyone seemed to be riveted, including Royce who was surprisingly wide awake. Her pastor concluded the short sermon with an altar call. Stretching out his hand, he offered an invitation, "There is never any reason for you to leave this church hungry. There's more food from where this came from, and you know what?"

The crowd responded, "What?"

"There are more gifts, too. If you want your presents, ask. Daddy, I want the box labeled Peace, I need two packages of Power. Need Joy? Yeah, it looks like that's here, too. C'mon. Today is a good day to ask. Repent first, confessing your sins, not to me, but to the Lord Jesus. Tell Him you're sorry. Ask Him for help.

"Once you've made up your mind, c'mon down for prayer. If you want to get rid of your filthy garments, let God wash your sins away in Jesus' name. He offers a full service makeover. He will wash, dry, press, and dress you Himself. C'mon now. There's no sense in letting these gifts go to waste."

After the benediction and witnessing three repentant souls get baptized in Jesus' name, members proceeded to the altar to joyously give their Christmas offerings to the deacons. Afterward, Royce reached for her hand. "Well, let's go unwrap gifts and create some more memories."

"Okay." She playfully wrinkled her nose. "After I feed you, then I'm putting you out, so you can go home and get some rest."

"My lady is kicking me out." They chuckled together as they put on their coats and exchanged holiday greetings with others as they walked to the car.

Back at Candace's house, Lindsay opened her gifts—all three of them—from Royce while Candace warmed up her turkey dinner. She hoped Royce liked the nature CDs she purchased for him to lull him to sleep and the few other small items from her and Lindsay.

She watched with amusement as her daughter

rewarded Royce with a death grip around his neck from her little arms for the 3-D twenty-five piece puzzle dollhouse that they had put together in record time. Lindsay bobbed her head up and down when Royce whispered something in her ear. Without speaking a word, her daughter skipped away. Royce patted the spot next to him on the love seat. "Your turn."

Chapter 27

Candace tried to hide her excitement. It had been five years since a man bought her any Christmas presents—gifts period. Her boss sending chocolates, cheese and nuts through the mail didn't count.

Once she made herself comfortable, Royce cooed, "Close your eyes."

The seat shifted seconds before she was ordered to open them. Candace's heart pounded at the sight of Royce on one knee. So what if it was cliche-ish.

"Baby, I love you," his husky voice began, "and that cute little girl in there." He paused to wipe at a tear that had escaped when she blinked. "I want you, Candace, and I need you and Lindsay to make my life complete. I'm ready to be your husband and her father. Marry me." Reaching into his pants pocket, he pulled out a tiny gift-wrapped box. "Say yes."

Her hand trembled as she pinched the tiny ribbon to untie it. Royce strong hand wrapped around hers to steady it. "Thanks," she said as her voice cracked.

Meticulously she unfolded the gift wrap that wasn't taped. She took a deep breath and they opened the blue velvet box together. "It's so beautiful."

"Like you….Will you marry me?"

Candace never thought this moment would come again. She never imagined she would ever utter, "Yes, I would be honored."

Royce slid the ring on her finger, then kissed her hand. He admired it before turning her hand over, then brushed his lips gently across her palm. "Thank you."

Closing her eyes, Candace leaned toward him. Royce graced her lips with a soft kiss. The sweetness lingered until she opened her eyes to meet his.

"You still want to send me home?"

"I guess you can stay fifteen minutes longer," she teased.

Lindsay appeared in the doorway. "Did Mommy say yes?" she asked excitedly as her new fiancé silently threatened to tickle her.

Had her daughter had been watching all along? She eyed Royce with a fake frown. "You were in cahoots with my daughter?"

"Yep. This is officially a family affair." He grinned. "Come on Lindsay, let's tickle Mommy."

Squealing, Candace pleaded for mercy. Royce wrapped her in his arms and Lindsay hugged her. She felt so loved. "As payback and because I care about my fiancé, I'm sending you home." "Yes, dear." After treating himself to a goodbye kiss, Royce strolled out the door, whistling. "I'm finally going to get me a wife."

Once Royce's tail lights had disappeared around the corner and Lindsay was occupied with the dollhouse that she and Royce had put together, Candace stared at the engagement ring. It was much bigger than the one Daniel had given her. Grabbing her cordless phone, she headed to her bedroom and closed the door. She couldn't contain her excitement when Solae answered. "I got a diamond for Christmas."

"Me, too."

Candace did a praise dance for both of them. Two friends, two brothers and two weddings. This was better than that old musical, *Seven Brides for Seven Brothers*.

Epilogue

Six months later, Candace and Royce stood at the altar with their wedding party: Solae as her maid of honor, Lindsay, the adorable flower girl and Hershel, Royce's best man.

The sanctuary was packed with well-wishers, including a heavy dose of firefighters. When a group of them left in a hurry, she and Royce exchanged knowing glances.

Solae was teary eyed that Candace had beaten her to the altar twice, but thankfully her good friend's day was coming. Candace refocused. She was moments away from becoming Mrs. Royce Kavanaugh.

"Therefore what God has joined together, let no dishonest man or conniving woman put asunder," Pastor Alexander stated with a twist that had become customary for the nuptials he officiated. Her pastor took marriage very seriously and his pre-nuptial counseling proved that. Still, the look of surprise on Royce's face was amusing.

Jesus, help us to be faithful, true and discerning about who we let into our circle, Candace silently added.

"You may now kiss your bride," Pastor Alexander granted his permission with a nod.

About the Author

PAT SIMMONS is a self-proclaimed genealogy sleuth. She is passionate about researching her ancestors, then casting them in starring roles in her novels. She hopes her off-beat method will track down distant relatives who happen to pick up her books. She has been a genealogy enthusiast since her great-grandmother died at the young age of ninety-seven years old in 1988.

She describes the evidence of the gift of the Holy Ghost as an amazing, unforgettable, life-altering experience. She believes God is the author who advances the stories she writes.

Pat has a B.S. in mass communications from Emerson College in Boston, Massachusetts. She has worked in various media positions in radio, television, and print for more than twenty years. Currently, she oversees the media publicity for the annual RT Booklovers Conventions.

She is the author of nine single titles and several eBook novellas. Her awards include *Talk to Me*, ranked #14 of Top Books in 2008 that Changed Lives by *Black Pearls Magazine*. She is a two-time recipient of the Romance Slam

Jam Emma Rodgers Award for Best Inspirational Romance for *Still Guilty* (2010) and *Crowning Glory* (2011), and the first recipient of the Katherine D. Jones Award for grace and humility as an author. Her bestselling novels include *Guilty of Love* and the Jamieson Legacy series: *Guilty by Association*, *The Guilt Trip*, and *Free from Guilt*. *The Acquittal* was her 2013 release; *No Easy Catch* is her 2014 release.

Pat has converted her sofa-strapped, sports-fanatical husband into an amateur travel agent, untrained bodyguard, and GPS-guided chauffeur. They have a son and daughter.

Pat's interviews include numerous appearances on radio, television, blogtalk radio, blogs, and feature articles.

Visit www.patsimmons.net or email her at authorpatsimmons@gmail.com

Snail mail: Pat Simmons, P O Box 1077, Florissant, MO 63031

A special thank you for choosing *Stopping Traffic,* Book 1 in the Love at the Crossroads series. I hope you will continue with Book II: *A Baby for Christmas,* Solae and Hershel's story. You will loved it!

And please take a few minutes to post a review. Thank you in advance.

Pat Simmons

Other Christian titles include:

The Guilty series
Book I: *Guilty of Love*
Book II: *Not Guilty of Love*
Book III: *Still Guilty*

The Guilty Parties series
Book I: *The Acquittal*
Book II: *The Confession,*
Fall 2015

The Jamieson Legacy
Book I: *Guilty by Association*
Book II: *The Guilt Trip*
Book III: *Free from Guilt*

The Carmen Sisters
Book I: *No Easy Catch*
Book II: *In Defense of Love*

Making Love Work Anthology
Book I: *Love at Work*
Book II: *Words of Love*
Book III: *A Mother's Love*

Love at the Crossroads
Book I: *Stopping Traffic*
Book II: *A Baby for Christmas*
Book III: *The Keepsake*
Book IV: *What God Has for Me*

Single titles
Crowning Glory
Talk to Me
Her Dress (novella)

Holiday titles
Love for the Holidays
(Three Christian novellas)
A Christian Christmas
A Christian Easter
A Christian Father's Day
A Woman After David's Heart (Valentine's Day)
Christmas Greetings

LOVE AT THE CROSSROADS SERIES

STOPPING TRAFFIC, *Book I of Love at the Crossroads series.* Candace Clark has a phobia about crossing the street, and for good reason. As fate would have it, her daughter's principal assigns her to crossing guard duties as part of the school's Parent Participation program. With no choice in the matter, Candace be-grudgingly accepts her stop sign and safety vest, then reports to her designated crosswalk. Once Candace is determined to overcome her fears, God opens the door for a blessing, and Royce Kavanaugh enters into her life, a firefighter built to rescue any damsel in distress. When a spark of attraction ignites, Candace and Royce soon discover there's more than one way to stop traffic.

A BABY FOR CHRISTMAS, *Book II of the Love at the Crossroads series.* Yes, diamonds are a girl's best friend, but in Solae Wyatt-Palmer's case, she desires something more valuable. Captain Hershel Kavanaugh is a divorcee and the father of two adorable little boys. Solae has never been married and longs to be a mother. Although Hershel showers her with expensive gifts, his hesitation about proposing causes Solae to walk and never look back. As the holidays approach, Hershel must convince Solae that she has everything he could ever want for Christmas.

THE KEEPSAKE, *Book III Love at the Crossroads series.* Until death us do part...or until Desiree walks away. Desiree "Desi" Bishop is devastated when she finds evidence of her husband's affair. God knew she didn't get married only to one day have to stand before a judge and file for a divorce. But Desi wants out no matter how much her heart says to forgive Michael. That isn't easier said than done. She sees God's one acceptable reason for a divorce as the only opt-out clause in her marriage. Michael Bishop is a repenting man who loves his wife of three years. If only...he had paid attention to the red flags God sent to keep him from falling into the devil's snares. But Michael didn't and he had fallen. Although God had forgiven him instantly when he repented, Desi's forgiveness is moving as a snail's pace. In the end, after all the tears have been shed and forgiveness granted and received, the couple learns that some marriages are worth keeping

LOVE FOR THE HOLIDAYS SERIES

A CHRISTIAN CHRISTMAS, *Book I of Love for the Holidays anthology.* Christian's Christmas will never be the same for Joy Knight if Christian Andersen has his way. Not to be confused with a secret Santa, Christian and his family are busier than Santa's elves making sure the Lord's blessings are distributed to those less fortunate by Christmas day. Joy is playing the hand that life dealt her, rearing four children in a home that is on the brink of foreclosure. She's not looking for a handout, but when Christian rescues her in the checkout line; her niece thinks Christian is an angel. Joy thinks he's just another man who will eventually leave, disappointing her and the children. Although Christian is a servant of the Lord, he is a flesh and blood man and all he wants for Christmas is Joy Knight. Can time spent with Christian turn Joy's attention from her financial woes to the real meaning of Christmas—and true love?

A CHRISTIAN EASTER, Book II Love for the Holidays anthology, How to celebrate Easter becomes a balancing act for Christian and Joy Andersen and their four children. Chocolate bunnies, colorful stuffed baskets and flashy fashion shows are their competition. Despite the enticements, Christian refuses to succumb without a fight. And it becomes a tug of war when his recently adopted ten year-old daughter, Bethani, wants to participate in her friend's Easter tradition.

Christian hopes he has instilled Proverbs 22:6, into the children's heart in the short time of being their dad.

A CHRISTIAN FATHER'S DAY, Book III Love for the Holidays anthology. Three fathers, one Father's Day and four children. Will the real dad, please stand up. It's never too late to be a father—or is it? Christian Andersen was looking forward to spending his first Father's day with his adopted children---all four of them. But Father's day becomes more complicated than Christian or Joy ever imagined. Christian finds himself faced with living up to his name when things don't go his way to enjoy an idyllic once a year celebration. But he depends on God to guide him through the journey.

MAKING LOVE WORK SERIES

 **Making Love Work, Book 1: A MOTHER'S LOVE.** To Jillian Carter, it's bad when her own daughter beats her to the altar. She became a teenage mother when she confused love for lust one summer. Despite the sins of her past, Jesus forgave her and blessed her to be the best Christian example for Shana. Jillian is not looking forward to becoming an empty-nester at thirty-nine. The old adage, she's not losing a daughter, but gaining a son-in-law is not comforting as she braces for a lonely life ahead. What she doesn't expect is for two men to vie for her affections: Shana's biological father who breezes back into their lives as a redeemed man and practicing Christian. Not only is Alex still goof looking, but he's willing to right the wrong he's done in the past. Not if Dr. Dexter Harris has anything to say about it. The widower father of the groom has set his sights on Jillian and he's willing to pull out all the stops to woo her. Now the choice is hers. Who will be the next mother's love?

Making Love Work, Book 2 : LOVE AT WORK. How do two people go undercover to hide an office romance in a busy television newsroom? In plain sight, of course. Desiree King is an assignment editor at KDPX-TV in St. Louis, MO. She dispatches a team to wherever breaking news happens. Her focus is to stay ahead of the competition. Overall, she's easy-going, respectable, and compassionate. But when it comes to dating a fellow coworker, she refuses to cross that professional line. Award-winning investigative reporter Bryan Mitchell makes life challenging for Desiree with his thoughtful gestures, sweet notes, and support. He tries to convince Desiree that as Christians, they could show coworkers how to blend their personal and private lives without compromising their morals.

Making Love Work, Book 3: WORDS OF LOVE. Call it old fashion, but Simone French was smitten with a love letter. Not a text, email, or Facebook post, but a love letter sent through snail mail. The prose wasn't the corny roses-are-red-and-violets-are-blue stuff. The first letter contained short accolades for a job well done. Soon after, the missives were filled with passionate words from a man who confessed the hidden secrets of his soul. He revealed his unspoken weaknesses, listed his uncompromising desires, and unapologetically noted his subtle strengths. Yes, Rice Taylor was ready to surrender to love. *Whew.* Closing her eyes, Simone inhaled the faint lingering smell of roses on the beige plain stationery. She had a testimony. If anyone would listen, she would proclaim that love was truly blind.

TESTIMONY: *IF I SHOULD DIE BEFORE I WAKE.*

It is of the LORD's mercies that we are not consumed, because His compassions fail not. They are new every morning, great is Thy faithfulness. Lamentations 3:22-23, God's mercies are sure; His promises are fulfilled; but a dawn of a new morning is God' grace. If you need a testimony about God's grace, then If I Should Die Before I Wake will encourage your soul. Nothing happens in our lives by chance. If you need a miracle, God's got that too. Trust Him. Has it been a while since you've had a testimony? Increase your prayer life, build your faith and walk in victory because without a test, there is no testimony.

HER DRESS. (Stand alone) Sometimes a woman just wants to splurge on something new, especially when she's about to attend an event with movers and shakers. Find out what happens when Pepper Trudeau is all dressed up and goes to the ball, but another woman is modeling the same attire.

At first, Pepper is embarrassed, then the night gets interesting when she meets Drake Logan. *Her Dress* is a romantic novella about the all too common occurrence—two women shopping at the same place. Maybe having the same taste isn't all bad. Sometimes a good dress is all you need to meet the man of your dreams.

The Guilty Series

Kick Off

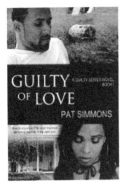

When do you know the most important decision of your life is the right one?

Reaping the seeds from what she's sown; Cheney Reynolds moves into a historic neighborhood in Ferguson, Missouri, and becomes a reclusive. Her first neighbor, the incomparable Mrs. Beatrice Tilley Beacon aka Grandma BB, is an opinionated childless widow. Grandma BB is a self-proclaimed expert on topics Cheney isn't seeking advice— everything from landscaping to hip-hop dancing to romance. Then there is Parke Kokumuo Jamison VI, a direct descendant of a royal African tribe. He learned his family ancestry, African history, and lineage preservation before he could count. Unwittingly, they are drawn to each other, but it takes Christ to weave their lives into a spiritual bliss while He exonerates their past indiscretions.

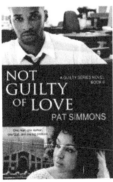

One man, one woman, one God and one big problem. Malcolm Jamieson wasn't the man who got away, but the man God instructed Hallison Dinkins to set free. Instead of their explosive love affair leading them to the wedding altar, God diverted Hallison to the prayer altar during her first visit back to church in years.

Malcolm was convinced that his woman had loss her mind to break off their engagement. Didn't Hallison know that Malcolm, a tenth generation descendant of a royal African tribe, couldn't be replaced? Once Malcolm concedes that their relationship can't be savaged, he issues Hallison his own edict, "If we're meant to be with each other, we'll find our way back. If not, that means that there's a love stronger than what we had." His words begin to haunt Hallison until she begins to regret their break up, and that's where their story begins. Someone has to retreat, and God never loses a battle.

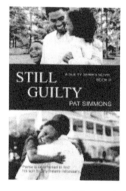

Cheney Reynolds Jamieson made a choice years ago that is now shaping her future and the future of the men she loves. A botched abortion left her unable to carry a baby to term, and her husband, Parke K. Jamison VI, is expected to produce heirs. With a wife who cannot give him a child, Parke vows to find and get custody of his illegitimate son by any means necessary. Meanwhile, Cheney's twin brother, Rainey, struggles with his anger over his ex-girlfriend's actions that haunt him, and their father, Dr. Roland Reynolds, fights to keep an old secret in the past.

Follow the paths of this family as they try to determine what God wants for them and how they can follow His guidance. Still Guilty by Pat Simmons is the third installment of the popular Guilty series. Read the other books in the series: Guilty of Love and Not Guilty of Love, and learn more about the Jamieson legacy in Guilty by Association, The Guilt Trip, and Free from Guilt. The Acquittal starts off the Guilty Parties series.

THE JAMIESON LEGACY SERIES

The Jamieson Legacy, Book I: *GUILTY BY ASSOCIATION.* How important is a name? To the St. Louis Jamiesons who are tenth generation descendants of a royal African tribe—everything. To the Boston Jamiesons whose father never married their mother—there is no loyalty or legacy. Kidd Jamieson suffers from the "angry" male syndrome because his father was an absent in the home, but insisted his two sons carry his last name. It takes an old woman who mingles genealogy truths and Bible verses together for Kidd to realize his worth as a strong black man. He learns it's not his association with the name that identifies him, but the man he becomes that defines him.

The Jamieson Legacy, Book II: *THE GUILT TRIP.* Aaron "Ace" Jamieson is living a carefree life. He's good-looking, respectable when he's in the mood, but his weakness is women. If a woman tries to ambush him with a pregnancy, he takes off in the other direction. It's a lesson learned from his absentee father that responsibility is optional. Talise Rogers has a bright future ahead of her. She's pretty and has no problem catching a man's eye, which is exactly what she does with Ace. Trapping Ace Jamieson is the furthest thing from Taleigh's mind when she learns she pregnant and Ace rejects her. "I want nothing from you Ace, not even your name." And Talise meant it.

The Jamieson Legacy, Book III: *FREE FROM GUILT.* It's salvation round-up time and Cameron Jamieson's name is on God's hit list. Although his brothers and cousins embraced God—thanks to the women in their lives—the two-degreed MIT graduate isn't going to let any woman take him down that path without a fight. He's satisfied with his career, social calendar, and good genes. But God uses a beautiful messenger, Gabrielle Dupree, to show him that he's in a spiritual deficit. Cameron learns the hard way that man's wisdom is like foolishness to God. For every philosophical argument he throws her way, Gabrielle exposes him to scriptures that makes him question his worldly knowledge.

THE GUILTY PARTIES SERIES

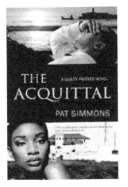

The Guilty Parties, Book I: *THE ACQUITTAL.* Two worlds apart, but their hearts dance to the same African drum beat. On a professional level, Dr. Rainey Reynolds is a competent, highly sought-after orthodontist. Inwardly, he needs to be set free from the chaos of revelations that make him question if happiness is obtainable. His father, the upstanding OB/GYN socialite is currently serving prison time after admitting his guilt in an old crime. His older sister refuses to move past the betrayal and attempts to use Rainey as a crutch, but her bitterness is only keeping the family at odds as his twin sister, Cheney Reynolds Jamieson, tries to rebuild a damaged relationship caused by decisions she made in the past. To get away from the drama, Rainey is willing to leave the country under the guise of a mission trip with Dentist Without Borders. Will changing his surroundings really change him? If one woman can heal his wounds, then he will believe that there is really peace after the storm.

Ghanaian beauty Josephine Abena Yaa Amoah returns to Africa after completing her studies as an exchange student in St. Louis, Missouri. She'll never forget the good friends she made while living there. She couldn't count Rainey in that circle because she rejected his advances for good causes. Josephine didn't believe in picking up the pieces as the rebound woman from an old relationship that Rainey seems to wear on his sleeve. Although her heart bleeds for his peace, she knows she must step back and pray for Rainey's surrender to Christ in order for God to acquit him of his self-inflicted mental torture. In the Motherland of Ghana, Africa, Rainey not only visits the places of his ancestors, will he embrace the liberty that Christ's Blood really does set every man free.

THE CARMEN SISTERS SERIES

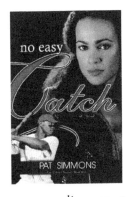

Book I: *No Easy Catch.* Shae Carmen hasn't lost her faith in God, only the men she's come across. Shae's recent heartbreak was discovering that her boyfriend was not only married, but on the verge of reconciling with his estranged wife. Humiliated, Shae begins to second guess herself as why she didn't see the signs that he was nothing more than a devil's decoy masquerading as a devout Christian man. St. Louis Outfielder Rahn Maxwell finds himself a victim of an attempted carjacking. The Lord guides him out of harms' way by opening the gunmen's eyes to Rahn's identity. The crook instead becomes infatuated fan and asks for Rahn's autograph, and as a good will gesture, directs Rahn out of the ambush!When the news media gets wind of what happened with the baseball player, Shae's television station lands an exclusive interview. Shae and Rahn's chance meeting sets in motion a relationship where Rahn not only surrenders to Christ, but pursues Shae with a purpose to prove that good men are still out there. After letting her guard down, Shae is faced with another scandal that rocks her world. This time the stakes are higher. Not only is her heart on the line, so is her professional credibility. She and Rahn are at odds as how to handle it and friction erupts between them. Will she strike out at love again? The Lord shows Rahn that nothing happens by chance, and everything is done for Him to get the glory.

Book II: *In Defense of Love.* Lately, nothing in Garrett Nash's life has made sense. When two people close to the U.S. Marshal wrong him deeply, Garrett expects God to remove them from his life. Instead, the Lord relocates Garrett to another city to start over, as if he were the offender instead of the victim.

Criminal attorney Shari Carmen is comfortable in her own skin—most of the time. Being a "dark and lovely" African-American sister has its challenges, especially when it comes to relationships. Although she's a fireball in the courtroom, she knows how to fade into the background and keep the proverbial spotlight off her personal life. But literal spotlights are a different matter altogether.

While playing tenor saxophone at an anniversary party, she grabs the attention of Garrett Nash. And as God draws them closer together, He makes another request of Garrett, one to which it will prove far more difficult to say "Yes, Lord."

Made in United States
Orlando, FL
25 September 2022

22776989R00104